POPULARITY

POPULARITY

Joseph Brown

VANTAGE PRESS
New York

This is a work of ficiton. Any similarity between
the names, characters, and places in this book and any
persons, living or dead, is purely coincidental.

Published by Vantage Press, Inc.
516 West 34th Street, New York, New York 10001

Manufactured in the United States of America
ISBN: 0-533-14050-1

Library of Congress Catalog Card No.: 01-126842

0 9 8 7 6 5 4 3 2 1

Contents

Acknowledgments

A special thanks to Mike, Kenny, Briana, and my father.

Introduction

Dear Diary,

His name was Mick Andrew Wilson. He was twenty-one years old when he left a year ago. He was struggling to afford a simple apartment that he never got to use. He worked for me and was also a really good human being. Mick had some problems but they were far from being harmful to others. Mick's best friend described him as a disturbed alcoholic that is only joyful when he met a stranger at a bar to drive him home. I think the reason for that is so he could get abusively drunk without the thought of crashing into a parked car or tree. He had no direction, but he was still a good man. In high school people called him nicknames like The Killer, Crazy, An Inspiration, The Beer Man, The Winner, The King, and The Role Model. I spoke to his best friend and from what he told me I believe that the outcomes of his life started to destroy him when he continued to cling on the thrill of being wanted. He was great at it, he loved the whole popularity contest. He loved the beer, the drugs, the fights, the football, the pranks, the girls, and most of all the parties. You couldn't blame him for not letting go, parties were fun and Mick was the best at it. He loved halfway killing himself every single weekend. Waking up with a blank memory, in a dark room and in a strange bed wondering where he was. Observing the situation and slapping himself in the head as he looked at the gorgeous looking female stranger located next to him. Quietly slipping out of the room and trying his best to get a ride home from people he met the night before. Driving in a car he's never seen before, telling his new friend he had no sexual motives for the past night. Being popular is what he did best.

POPULARITY

Being a Senior (Winner)

I was a senior in Burbank High School when my crazy life reached its most ludicrous peak. I started the first day of school with a greeting from more than half of my graduating class. They said hello like maybe I grew up with them like some kind of brother or sister. I did nothing for them except provide a place to get intoxicated with the knowledge that the authorities would never disrupt my party. The other half that didn't say hello were nerds, geeks, or the occasional new student.

Never suffering the ugly complexions of acne or any type of alien growths on my face, I never had problems with the opposite sex. Being the first day, I thought I would take advantage of the situation by asking out some of the attractive new girls, showing up to my school like some kind of rookies. Still, before I did that I thought it would be nice if I said hello to my true friends first.

The first person I bumped into was a freak. His name was Donny. I never really cared for Donny, but he was a friend with the people that I thought were worthy enough to hang out with me. So I allowed him the privilege of being seen with me. We walked down the hall while suffering through a bit of chitchat that I could have done without when we saw Bradley.

Bradley was an adventurer, big, tall, good-looking,

funny, kind of crazy, and every trait I desired people to see me with. He was the closest to me, the kind of person you could trust and out of all my friends Bradley most resembled me. Bradley was like a brother to me, he was the kind of companion you wouldn't leave behind in a war no matter how many people couldn't fit on a chopper.

After I met up with Brad and engaged myself in what happened the day before the first day of school, all of my friends just started to spring up. There was Bradley, Kenny, Travis, Jason, and his friend Donny. All of my favored associates had their highlights, which served in establishing their gracious right to hang out with me. Travis was kept around mainly for the entertainment. He was always making people laugh with a twist of madness and sometimes I questioned if he was really joking or if he was seriously crazy. Jason lived as my very own jackal that kept a large amount of mental issues in his pathetic mind receiving his joy in pranks and vandalism. Kenneth was the biggest pot dealer in the city and has dealt weed out as long as I have known him. He knew a lot of people that could make a lot of things happen, he ran the total amount of drugs in the city and could get any type of drug at anytime. Still, there were only about six of us and six people was all that was needed to run the student body sternly, but my five companions needed a general.

After I bumped into my associates, I kept a look out for the unsuspecting opposite sex whose greatest fear that day is not being able to talk to anyone, but first I had a class to attend.

Being a senior, I finished all of my difficult classes when I was a freshman and sophomore. My class schedule was filled with gym class and a required class the school made you take so people like me don't make a mockery of the education system.

I showed up for gym with an attractive female that I picked up on the way over to class. I was already educating her about a party that would take place in honor of the new school year, and that was when I saw the newest member of Burbank High. She was about my height, blonde hair, blues eyes, very slender, and very good looking. She was wearing a white T-shirt tucked into some jean cutoffs that traced the stunning gifts of her youth, and I had no choice but to introduce myself to this fine example of beauty. Girls of her disposition did not stay shy and single for long.

I started a topic of conversation that seemed most fitting for both of us, since when I opened the conversation this girl didn't stop talking until I wanted to break her scrawny little neck. I saw her lips moving but didn't really pay attention. I know what I wanted and didn't care how I got it. The more I comprehended the idea of my licentious acts the more I felt like bending her over right there in class. You see girls in the nineties wanted it just as much as guys, I wasn't about to be the one in punishing this poor sweet girl by not giving it to her. Her name was Jennifer.

After the dismissal of the first day of school, my friends roared me as a ladies man. I won a date with the newest and most attractive member of Burbank High. My companions had already heard rumors of this elegant trophy and would give up many of their past dates for a chance with this prize to be won.

After football practice I got home and informed my parents of my false destination. My father, never thinking that I could fulfill the horrible tasks that I was about to, trusted me and gave me money for dinner.

As I rushed down the stairs of my three-story niche I met my thoughts to my garage and chose a car of my choice. My parents had three high-class transportation vehicles that they all paid for and let me use whenever I felt like it. I never paid attention to the new 99 Toyota trucks that my parents drove. I needed a choice, a car that I could show off. I drove a red 420 LE BMW that my father paid for due to the sick act of his midlife crisis.

As I cruised to her house my friends no doubt were filling their microscopic minds with excitement of the sexual deeds that would later happen. Oh, how they wished they were standing in my shoes driving to her house. I of course expected a long caring and intimate relationship until of course she stopped giving it up. The single-minded thoughts of a mature brain would consider my strange everyday lifestyle a disgusted approach of looking at females, but when guys like me are put into perspective some of the ladies found themselves begging for it.

I pulled up to the house that matched the address given to me on the phone and parked on the long gravel driveway. I got out of my car to be confronted by the scarred settings of her corrupted domain. I asked myself how a girl that looked so good could live in a dump like this. The gravel driveway was actually her front yard. There were unwanted weeds that seemed to pop up every four feet. They had one creepy old tree that just seemed to take up space on the corner of her yard. There was an outlining sidewalk that was broken from the strong roots of this once living creature. The old house was no different from the other neighboring houses that ran parallel to Jennifer's. Paint chips barely hung onto wood that barely held together. The windows were covered with plastic that stuck on the dusty ripped screens from the year before. The house had no sidewalk leading to the front door and the front door had no step where there probably should have been one. There was a dirt patch in front of their door where a welcome mat used to lie.

I pushed the doorbell, but heard no ring so I tried the old fashioned way and knocked. I was afraid that if I hit the door too hard in this condition I would most likely break it in. My patience was disturbing me, as I awkwardly waited forever in front of this embarrassment. Just when I felt like sucking gasoline out of my car and putting this house out of its misery, the door swung wide.

The stunning reason for me standing here oozed out as if time ran in slow motion. Jennifer wore a black almost skin-tight shirt, and a blue mini skirt that looked like it was fitted for her body. In her right hand she carried a small brown purse and in her left a letterman's jacket that she was just slipping on. She apologized for making me wait and I apologized for not buying her flowers.

I believe I told her the recycled lie of tight expenses that never posted a problem for me since I had no bill that my parents wouldn't pay for.

I never bought food myself because my father believes that kids should never go hungry. I never found myself needing gas because when my car of choice didn't have enough I would decide on another vehicle until my parental counterparts paid for more. My place of employment, The Cinemax, was the largest movie theater in the city, so I never paid for a movie ticket and it meant that I could get anyone I desired into the giant projections of movie screens. This also proposed a factor in my popularity. All I needed to do to make a new friend was let a stranger in with no charge and get the person's name. As far as I could remember all I ever used my money for was alcoholic beverages which I gave out freely to those who showed up to my parties.

I opened the entrance of my candy-apple red BMW and gently let her in. With the car door still ajar I told her how magnificent she looked and with that she passed me a smile. As I walked around I caught the astonished look on her impressed face as she fiddled with all of the small switches and buttons of the most expensive item she had ever laid eyes on. I got behind the steering wheel and asked her if she would like to handle a small taste of a great car. Knowing the answer before she said it, she got out and we traded seats. Before I knew it the car was alive, then accelerated down the street like we were the only two left on the planet. As we rounded street corners, Jennifer portrayed a look of the virgin drivers that we all once were.

While flying down the black pavement we reached our freeway destination in a quick matter of time, and I questioned her if she wanted to see the movie or get some dinner first. In a quick simple response she asked where I wanted to eat. Her eyes widened as I suggested one of the most costly restaurants in the city. The slender looking mini skirt disagreed like she didn't want to taste the exquisite dining because of my economic class. She also complained that the delicacies could not be touched without a twenty-four hour waiting list. In a calm fashion I reached over and opened my glove box, pulling out my cellular phone. I switched on my communication device and phoned the destination of our soon-to-be meal. Asking to speak with my right arm man Bradley, I switched on the booming sound of my vehicle's stereo system and waited.

As Jennifer and I listened to the motivating sound of the new local band "Novatemp," I noticed the youthful gifts that pushed down on the black accelerating pedals of my racing car. Her tan legs ran out of her skirt and moved to the sound of what she replied her favorite band. I was slightly embarrassed, since I couldn't remember if she tried to talk to me while I was fixated at the perfect walking devices of the prize piece, as I was quickly awakened out of my sexual daydream, by Brad's answer. Trusting Bradley with my life, he would have a special table ready when I got there. Bradley never paid for movie tickets and I always got a seat at the finest restaurants in the city whenever I wanted.

Upon my arrival, the flooded number of people provided us with no parking spaces so we parked in the "employee only parking," as some of the workers presented an ugly look on their faces. Some of the brave workers were about to confront the unknown driver, as I opened my door and approached them with a smile. I knew all of the of-age buyers through Brad at a party I once assembled, and although I shunned the idea of hanging out with these low lives, I could always use another twenty-one year old to purchase me some more beer.

On the drive in I glanced at the endless line of people standing in one long row that seemed to never move. They were mostly just pathetic angry families led by fathers whose only joy in life comes when his stuck up disgraceful children share a quiet peaceful dinner with each other. I can't understand how parents could inch through life watching the disrespectful hooligans they spawned to replace themselves with, take over the family business like some kind of happy soap opera. Listening to a whole generation of father, son, and grandson mingle about how sick grandma was, is always the worst aspect of waiting in a line. Fortunately, I brought Jennifer through the back door, past the kitchen and straight to our waiting table located slightly in front of a small water fountain that resembled an angel.

I always try to present myself as a gentleman with small acts of kindness such as pulling out her chair that was straight across from me, then placing my napkin on my lap, and complimenting her with flattering statements. Small gestures like these showed my date that I wasn't the heartless barbarian that I really am.

I received a quick hello from most of the fellow high school workers and introduced my attractive friend to all who stopped to say hello. She loved the fact of her growing number of friends, but already knew my favorite companion Bradley, who gave me the quick speech about how he despised the trends of employment.

Waiting for the menus to arrive I asked her if I was winning the battle of making her feel special in playing my role as the perfect escort employee. Jokingly, she told me if the night pursues to end the way it started she would in no question marry me.

My intentions for Jennifer left for awhile, and focussed on the stunningly beautiful waitress that brought us our folded menus. The brunette wore a tight brown mini-skirt that her workplace considered a uniform. She also had on a matching brown apron that fit nice with her white blouse.

I tried to act as if I was paying attention to the boring on going conversation my date opened, as the attractive greeter walked back and forth serving others in a tired strut. Pretending not to notice the perfect example of the model worker as she passed glances in my direction, I looked at my forgotten date and signaled in a small gesture that we were ready to order. I tried not to look at the server while she tried to straighten her hair and brush off loose food before she took my order, thinking maybe if she presented herself nice enough I would dump the lucky girl in front of me then chase after her.

After we ordered it was routine for a woman to powder her nose and make sure her looks met her expectations. Knowing this rule of dating I thought I would take advantage of the situation and introduce myself to the girl that Bradley forgot to.

The girl's name was Michelle. She was a junior and was also a new member of Burbank High. She brought it to my attention that she had already heard of who I was and knew of my party that would take place right after the Varsity football game on Friday. I told her that the party would either drown my sorrows of loss or celebrate the victories of winning, but either way I was getting drunk.

Giving my next victory in the making an assumption of wanting her more than the tan curves I walked in with, I told her I wanted her to make attendance at the intoxicated celebration. Michelle was convinced that I cared for her and knew that my real date would return shortly, so as a kind mistress she exited the short romantic scene. The envious mind of a male would say *stop cheating and let others experience the fine taste of the most choice females in the school,* but I was not yet committed to any lasting relationships, therefore how could I cheat? Besides most of my fellow classmates would not know what to do with the opposite sex, and most definitely corrupt the mind of the poor sweet girl causing her to think of herself as the drooling ugly monster that nobody wanted. This is all enough reason for me to reach up the skirts of women with such potential and caress the most uncharted part of the female anatomy, then giving them what they want.

When Jennifer finally returned the food was waiting to be devoured. I don't recall what she ordered, but I remember she brought up my financial problem, as she limited herself to what she was going to eat. We did not talk much during the meal and tried to finish as quickly as we could without being rude. In no matter of time both of our plates were completely empty, and I asked her if she wanted anything else. I didn't need to ask her knowing the size of the meal she just ate, but if I knew she was going to say yes, I wouldn't of asked. I paid the bill then said good-bye to all of the familiar faces I passed on the way in. This time exiting out the front door, I passed the endless line of upset people waiting to get in. I couldn't help laughing to myself, as I recognized the same families standing in the same location now hungrier and twice as angry. We found the car and I gently helped her in.

I was now behind the wheel and speeding down the moonlit road questioning what movie was most desirable to her. Stuck in the sad economic class that could not provide a television for the abused lifestyles of this deprived woman, she did not know what was showing. Telling me to choose for her I thought it would be a nice gesture to pick a movie with some intelligence without being too obvious in creating the mood. When we got there I again observed another meaningless line of people whose goal is to inch their way inside only to wait for another line, and after paying for overpriced popcorn they can finally watch their movie. Luckily, I worked here so I brought Jennifer through the back door as she looked at her date with an impressive stare, hoping I wasn't some kind of Mafia leader.

Once again I showed off this lucky piece introducing her to everyone who worked that night. I led Jennifer into the black quiet room that projected the movie, finding two seats located in the front rows. The room seemed small since all of the lights were turned off, and you could not see the red tapestries that lined the outside of the room. There were over three hundred chairs in this portable Hollywood production, it also seated an average of one hundred people a night, but through the endless space of blackness I couldn't see a single chair. That is why I purchased popcorn and other refreshments before I entered this black labyrinth.

Before I let Jennifer sit next to me, I laid out my arm to slip around her once she sat down, but still I presented myself as the kind date, asking her if she was offended if I added some protection during the suspenseful scenes of this dramatic show. She sat and rested her head on my shoulder while gently running her hands around my stomach. I could smell the hypnotizing fumes of her sweet perfume, as I started to fall asleep.

I woke up to the image of a young veteran that fought for his last breath of fresh air, as an attractive nurse fought and cried for his life. I knew that I chose the correct movie when Jennifer wiped her tears away from her face, knowing that after a little more suspense and crying, Jennifer would need someone to cheer her up. Oh, how I had fine plans for delivering this nice girl from deep depression to the glowing feelings of an experienced winner.

I fell in and out of sleep through the whole boring film, as I watched a pathetic nurse cry over a man like they grew up with each other in an impossible dream life, thought up by some love struck fool whose only desire was to die before his wife so maybe he wouldn't be heartbroken if she died first. I never did understand the love scenario of keeping together and sticking with one person. If one person could give another a reason to live then two people should make one even more ecstatic, and that brings me to conclude my theory, the more the merrier.

After the long ongoing battle of love and war, I asked Jennifer if she wanted to watch the sunset. I was extremely excited to finally get to the point at hand. I wanted to hurry and fulfill the reason of the long boring day, but I knew I didn't need to rush since one way or another my goal was inevitable. She loved everything about me, I was kind, good-looking, polite, rich, and I had connections.

I tried to calm myself down, as I sped down the road to the familiar deserted destination I brought all of my lucky dates. I had no idea what to call this concealed place of youthful love and reoccurring acts of sex, but it had a perfect place to park while presenting a great view of the sunset shining over the huge city.

Still in the car, I asked her to rate the night as compared to her past dates, while watching the golden sun sink below the mountains waking up a new day for others. She did not question the fact that I presented her with the most exciting night she has ever lived through and with that my lips pressed up against hers. I squeezed the inside of her thigh, as I felt her lips close down on my intruding tongue. Somewhere between kissing and stripping off her skirt, I relocated on top of her while laying the seat back to give the sense of lying down. I took off her white silk panties and she slowly unzipped my jeans. I won.

The Normal Day for the Elite

The following morning is always a mixture of thoughts, thinking about the previous night of cheating a pregnancy. Pregnancy never forced myself into a nervous reaction because I just could not bring myself to care about the subject. If my previous victories hated the idea of a child, then they would responsibly supply themselves with a type of birth-control.

I woke up the next morning looking at the white background of my bedroom ceiling. Great memories filled my mind as I got up to take a refreshing shower. Passing my mother, she complimented me on how happy and cheerful I looked, thinking if only she knew the sweet pleasures I previously participated in. After a night of such great exhilaration no stressful obstacles could ever bring a person down.

I hopped in the refreshing shower, feeling how much the hot streams of water reminded me of the warm sweat that ran off Jennifer's body when she shook just before the unexplainable orgasmic feeling grew to a climax, and she started to moan. She said losing her virginity to me was worth holding out for and would enjoy seeing me again. I had no objections to a second night of passion and romance, but after I was finished with my naked acts I didn't need her so I drove her home. Before she got out of my car I don't know if she believed me when I said I loved her, but as long as she wanted it again, it didn't matter.

I stepped out of the shower and started with all of my basic morning routines. I started to brush my teeth, when my mother yelled through the door, saying she had to work early and breakfast was on the kitchen table.

She worked at a day-care center, while my father spent his day making phone calls for his own insurance company. I love my parents, but I hate the fact that they had the most embarrassing jobs anyone could possibly get. Insurance was not a profession that I desired to go into no matter how good a job my father said it was, and cleaning up after hundreds of brats for a living is a sad way of saying, I couldn't get a job at Macdonald's. I never gave my future a lot of thought, but I could of guaranteed I wouldn't be sitting behind a boring desk making phone calls to accident-prone people or changing diapers while some kid you've never seen before urinates in your face. I never did understand how local heroes like myself, came from the lame counterparts that gave birth to me.

Of-age buyers force themselves to stay at home because they think it's responsible. They own the nicest cars and biggest houses, but never throw parties. They make enough money to retire but for some strange reason they keep saving. A wild weekend for my parents was renting a motel just so their only son can't hear them moan and scream. They did this frequently and it saddened me on how my parents turned themselves into everything that I hated. I made a small promise to myself that committing suicide was the more pleasing alternative to this sick lifestyle.

I started to make my way downstairs when I

caught the mouth-watering aroma of eggs and sausage. I grabbed the white plate as I indulged myself in the fulfilling smell that would once again revive my growling stomach. I carried the plate over to my black leather couch, placing it on the shiny crystal coffee table my parents forbid me to eat on. I turned on the television set, zoning out in one of my favorite past times. Television was in no doubt the invention of an incredible genius. If there was anyone I could relate my life with, it was the colorful characters on the television set. No one led boring lives and stayed at home just waiting to die of old age. People always had things to do and places to go, but one of the best things about television was being able to switch the station if a show was boring. There was always a show to entertain me when I was watching television at my house. One of my father's finer decisions was to purchase a satellite dish just so his heir could be raised properly from our big screen TV. I sometimes cringe at the thought of deprived youth that are not raised on the same television channels that I take for granted.

One of the downfalls of television was losing track of time. I just realized that I was already late for my first period class. Grabbing all of my school gear I was quickly out the door and in my car. In a panicked state I drove down the street while convincing myself that nothing could prevent my tardiness.

I then slowed down and started to enjoy the nice scenery of my rich growing neighborhood. I passed Bradley's house, which was right down the street from mine. It was constructed similar to mine except mine was blue and his house was green. We both lived in three-story complexes except we were hardly ever home due to football and other extracurricular activities. If my friends did anything at a house we did it at mine mainly because of my pool table, swimming pool, big screen TV, the two acre backyard, and my parents were never home on the weekends. A brown wooden fence that prevented the neighbors from seeing how big a party I was throwing surrounded my backyard. I also allowed people to park back there since my parents nosey neighboring friends would call the authorities on me once the driveway was full, but the police didn't ever pose a problem in my neighborhood unless they were notified by an anonymous person. I lived in such a wealthy atmosphere the police department automatically assumed anything growing up in such a prestige manner couldn't possibly cause any reason for them to be concerned. Cops usually wasted their time patrolling in the poor dirty gutters of the city, as the town's elite celebrated with only the small fear that my abnormal lifeless neighbors might call the authorities on me. I think it is sad that my neighbors are filled with so much jealousy and boredom that they entertain themselves by going out of their way to deprive a bunch of harmless kids of America's favorite past time, partying.

Pulling up to the parking lot I asked myself, why go? Deep down inside I knew I was too clever to be forced anymore useless education since I was smarter than the average and saw how the world ran. I didn't mind my gym classes, but I knew my world history class would be a term I could easily do without. Sitting in a desk listening to some old man read out of a book that could be read twice as fast if it interested us.

The problem with the history taught in school is that teachers don't teach the correct literature. I find George Washington an insulting waste of time, when I could be taught the ways of Bob Marley or Dennis Rodman. I think that anyone that encouraged the knowledge of the Gettysburg Address is a sick twisted individual that would be dealt with to the fullest of my power.

This is where my lifelong enemy plays a huge role in my school career. His name was Steven Parker. He was a 4.0 student from the day he was born, and was fascinated by the ugly natures of education. I hated him and have proven it ever since kindergarten. This nerd promoted the learning environment into his life and actually tried not to party. He liked the strange ways of intellect and even when homework was not assigned he would spend his filthy time in writing what jokes I have played on him in his diary.

The doomed being had thick black glasses that sat on his acne-covered face and wore clothing that I first saw on him as a sophomore. He had brown hair and carried a revolting smell that could easily be solved if the geek ever showered.

I remember a humorous mocking experiment that I once participated in, that proves this theory of his rancid stench. With a bit of sneakiness I drew a small dash mark on the band of his disgusting underwear representing a day. After reaching twelve dash marks he finally showed mercy to those with sensitive noses, and changed his poverty stricken britches.

I was more than happy to find out he had some of the same classes as me, just so I could convince him that his computer ways served no purpose in life. I was kind of curious to see what this nerd did in his spare time, since the reputation I so humbly gave him denied him conversation with anyone in the school. No one ever invited him to a party and I never heard his name come up with conversing with the opposite sex. I now know that the riotous exists in the world and plays a cruel joke on the wicked, preventing it from succeeding in life.

The bell rang out telling kids it was lunchtime. Lunch was probably the busiest time of the day for the fast food establishments, and it also served as a break for the delicate minds of the high school environment. Lunch was served at school, but I'd rather be dead than be caught sitting amongst the carless, talking about Star Trek and comic books.

Only the hip ate out, but there were still a number of nerds that were accidentally given the right to drive an automobile. People sat with their pathetic little groups trying to make each other laugh at their own sorry little inside jokes. I could sit with anyone that I desired, but today I thought it would be a great gesture to take out Jennifer, since I trembled at the mental picture of her being caught with a disturbed horny little freshman that couldn't drive.

It took me a while to find her, but when I did she made it all worthwhile, once again impressing me with her tight blue jeans and tank top shirt. She quickly gave me a hug and told me of the horrified thoughts of eating at school.

After I located her I bumped into my buddies, and decided to follow them to our familiar place of eating. It was just a local 50s-style hamburger business called Snyder's, which was run by a whole family of hard workers. They served the best burgers in town and kept alive big rock stars of the past. They played nothing but oldies, which I thought was cool, and had pictures of Elvis Presley plastered all over the walls. There were also pictures of different past legends that looked over every single booth, and on every table laid a classic miniature jukebox that listed all of the music.

When we arrived at the location the place was packed but I still managed to get the seat next to the James Dean poster that my friends so thoughtfully reserved for me. People stared at me wondering whose hand I held, as I sat Jennifer down and asked what she found most craving to eat. After I found out what we both wanted I followed the checkered floor all the way up to the back of the line, as the eyes of the envious finally questioned the never-before-seen girl, who clung on to me marking her as property. I referred to her as mine, knowing that if anyone was foolish enough to act out their understandable sexual attraction they would be confronted with a severe beating fulfilled by a number of my loyal friends.

After finally giving my order to the cashier I walked my way back finding my booth was surrounded by a number of female classmates, asking the new girl questions and explaining how lucky she was automatically assuming we were together. I politely asked one of Jennifer's new jealous friends to shove over a bit so I could share the seat with her as everyone stared at me expecting an explanation of why I chased after this girl and not one of them. I remember falsely saying, "We've only been on one date, but I feel like I love her," when I really meant, "I went out with her because I couldn't brag about getting some from a disgusting cow like you."

After lunch, I entered my third period class with all of my high school chums excited to goof off during one of the first induction days. The class warmed up everyday with two laps around the track, then normally did anything that was athletically active, except today. Today the gym instructor wanted to measure our stamina by making us do some rope climbing.

The girls usually received the job of paperwork because the gym instructor was always the football or wrestling coach. If the gym instructor was a volleyball coach the girls would have strained themselves for a stronger body while the coach motivated his soldiers into doing activities he could never do. A huge fight could go unnoticed if the coach caught my companions and I not exercising. When a rule like this was in power, I found it more tempting to do exactly the opposite of what the coach planned us to do.

After warming up, we all stood around the white thick rope waiting to climb up faster than anyone else in the class, showing off like it was some kind of iron man contest. The strong old rope hung from the middle of the gym, and was parallel to each of the basketball hoops that were hung from walls at each end of the gym. The basketball hoops had two gray doors on each side of them serving as an exit and entrance to the locker rooms.

One by one an excited student jumped up eager to determine that they were the strongest in the class and tried to prove it by the velocity one climbs up the rope. I watched the competitors climb, while mingling with some of my lady-friends, when Bradley proved himself the strongest. I couldn't remember his time since all I could concentrate on were the tight attractive workout clothing that were trying their best to gain my attention, but I had no goals of proving myself the strongest in the class.

Somewhere in the back of my head I knew I could easily climb up the swiftest no matter how much my favorite companion indulged himself in small victory dances. After he finished his silly heckles I stood up and walked toward the meaningless effort that made people think so highly of themselves. I looked the strong white rope up and down, while looking back at the open space of girls I had just left. I then stood aside while my right arm yelled out his quickest score, and dared me to do better.

In a quick act of courage, Steven Parker threw off his glasses, and began to inch his way up the rope. At this moment all of my friends started to cry out in a humorous state of mocking laughter as the sad nerd used all of his power to now stay in one place. I then knew there was no other alternative to what I was about to do.

I grabbed on to his white sweats, ripped them down all the way. I observed the dignity of this embarrassed nerd, as it came to my attention that the cotton fabrics of Steven's underwear were also held in my hand. The class paused for a couple of seconds to figure out what exactly was going on when they fell down in laughter. Steven still clung to the rope when I started to grab his feet and rip him off. I yanked him off the rope and he hit the ground with an enormous thud. There was a thin line between laughter and pain when my classmates held their stomachs, as I dragged the half-naked body of Steven across the gym floor.

Entertainment comes in different shapes and sizes, but the fun I had when I punished Steven couldn't be measured. I never attended much church, but I knew that God smiled upon me because everyone wanted to be me. I ran the school almost knowing God sent me to this world as a late judge or to punish the wicked. The wicked are a sneaky and cunning folk filled with evil plans of temptation that quickly attract the end of the world. I didn't read much of the Bible, but I know that God marks the wicked the way God marked Cain for killing his own brother. Nerds live their disgusting lives with no manners, no dignity, and no respect. People can easily see this in the way they present themselves and the lifestyles they live, but I was not about to stand around doing nothing while the evil plans of Satan are fulfilled.

It seemed like it lasted forever, as I was giving Steven his sentence although it couldn't have been a couple of seconds. I dropped Steven's leg and started to take off in a heckling sprint, as I heard the sharp cold sound of my gym instructor's whistle cut through the air followed by a long period of silence. Everyone quickly looked at me questioning my next spontaneous move. With Steven's clothes still in my hand I walked over and tossed him his dignity. As I looked upon his face I noticed the little freak started to cry probably just to get me in more trouble than I was already in. The teacher started to scream out laps, as he nursed the pathetic excuse of a man up onto his feet, while walking over to the male locker rooms.

I went outside to start my running when my friends joined me. They had no part of this school crime but as usual the teacher automatically assumed my friends helped me follow out with this simple act of fun and games. The gym instructor was told by my alleged soldiers and others from the class that my disciples served no operatives in this silly crime of ignorance, but nothing could change the single-minded decision of my football coach. This only made matters worse for Mr. Parker, since my associates were already conversing about plans of revenge. You could almost see the anger grow inside my most fond followers, as they talked about different ideas of getting even. All suggested ideas of revenge were laughed upon, but my favorite outrageous and impossible idea sprouted from Bradley, as he wheezed in oxygen from the constant run.

He shared his humorous story on how we could strip off his clothing and then blindfold him. We could then smear raspberry jam all over his skinny body, while laying him on top of a giant anthill giving the bugs a less than worthy meal to snack on. Meanwhile, someone could pass out flyers presenting the coordinates of this glorious sight showing the humor that is brought upon the wicked.

After about forty-five minutes of running we were told to come inside, and apologize to our forever enemy, then think about how horrible I treated Stevie. My coach did not realize I had no regrets for my actions and I probably would have done worse if he didn't interrupt us.

My buddies cursed the name of our PE teacher, as they crept inside pondering sweet deeds of heckling they could do to get even with that weak boy. Just before we reached the door of the gym I concocted a theory of an insult that was so simple, one of the educated minds would congratulate me of such fine thinking. People of the weak-minded would find my ways of entertainment very sick and unjust, but for some unexplained reason I had to, like some kind of drug I was addicted in the funny harassments of this strange parasite. He was nothing. I was everything, and oh how I loved the sweet beatings of Mr. Parker.

We walked in, and out onto the basketball court, finding that the freak was standing next to our coach fully clothed and not as sad. Surrounding them were the rest of the class, as they waited for their hero to apologize to the well-known geek that shed a tear because someone had to hurt his precious feelings.

I felt like kicking him right in the face. This guy couldn't stand there without sending out this weird aura that cried out, "I'm a nerd and you have the God-given right to beat me."

I walked over and said I was sorry, then reaching out my hand to show it was over, ever so wanting to just squeeze his hand until I heard the crunching sound of his wimpy bones. Knowing Steven he would probably retaliate back by a girlish cry, as I would laugh straight into his acne-stricken face. I could make myself laugh just thinking of the fantastic accidents that could happen to Mr. Parker. If I were to compare this geek to anything that walked the earth, he would probably serve a greater purpose if he were a mushroom growing off the manure of a tick-infested animal. If I could I would strip off his clothing then tie his body on top of the flagpole, and leave him swinging over a giant pile of cow manure just so he learned that he wasn't a man.

While walking to the locker room to change the coach gave me a huge lecture that probably served as a wake up call for freaks everywhere.

The coach couldn't punish us too hard, since we all played football for him and held a huge piece in winning. He cherished the football game like it was a one way ticket to heaven and he treated me as his son. This was an area that I found suitably normal to crave since I knew how much I wanted to be victorious in the upcoming game, dreaming of the cheering fans as they wished they found more time and effort to play football with me.

When we got into the locker room, I found Steven was already cleansing himself with about twenty other males. The shower room was laced with white tile and had about twenty-five showerheads sticking out of the walls. There were about two hundred red lockers built in rows right on top of each other. These rows faced other rows, and my locker was located next to all of my buddies. They were now changing, as I consulted with them of my outstanding mission against the small weakling that just exited out the door.

After hearing my plan, my friends agreed the simple hypothesis was a sure proof method that would bring Steven to once again believe he didn't have the right to socialize with other humans. I let out a small excited laugh, as I pondered the operation, slipping on my blue jeans. I threw on my shirt and shut my locker door, then rushed over to one of the unused stalls that provided a toilet. I didn't have to relieve myself but I forced out every bit of human waste I had in me. When I was finished, I left the remains in the white toilet unflushed and allowed my waiting friends to do their deeds in the same infected bowl of water, as we all laughed at the never before seen situation we currently underwent.

After they were finished I quickly went over the plan making sure they didn't screw it up no matter how easy this school beating seemed. I peeked out the locker room to locate the main objective to our plan, when Bradley pointed out he merely stood on the other side of our locker room door, not suspecting he was the key factor in another humble prank. Oh, it was too good to be true.

I opened the door and put my hand around his mouth, disabling him of speech, while forcing him back; my friends grabbed his aggravating limbs, as they moved about in a fight to be free. We carried Steven over to our disgusting porcelain weapon, as he started to scream out even with my hands over his mouth. We raised his head first over the rancid toilet, as male classmates started to fill in and surround the loud commotion with loud abusive laughter. All of us started to laugh as we dropped him in, then observing his whole head stain with brown filth, and with his feet still held in the air I swung as hard as I could, nailing the disgrace in the stomach, then knocking the wind out of him. This caused him to open his mouth filling it up with the worst taste he had ever felt and gasping for oxygen that was replaced by human defecation. We could see him try to suck in the human waste like it was air, using the little amount of oxygen he had received to beg us for mercy. Then maybe we would stop and the laughter would cease, then we could all return to class like nothing ever happened, but it could not and would not happen in that manner.

Seconds before Steven suffocated to death on the last transformations of digestion we pulled him out letting him breathe in the air that he didn't deserve, and watched him start to cry like the little sissy that he was. He crunched over in a ball to cough out all of the human sludge that was inhaled into his lungs, as the brown waste dripped off his hair then onto his clothing. I watched with about twenty others, as the freak started to stand up and head for the sink, moaning in his sorry retaliation of tears.

The school bell rang to note the ending of our third period class, but it didn't seem that Steven would be attending the rest of the school day, knowing there was nothing he could do to wash out the disgusting brown stains fixed in his clothing. The sissy tried to wipe his tears but just spread the filth on his hands, crying out in a quiet voice "why," he said after every breath of air that was slowed by the self-inflicted insults of crying. I stayed to watch the humorous situation when everyone else in the room left for their next class and when I was alone with humanity's disgrace I struck Steven straight in the corner of his face knocking him to the ground, ever so happy to see that justice had been served.

I finished school with the feeling that I was a good person. Oh, how great I felt dealing with the wicked in a way that made them realize who was the dominant one. I know the gates of heaven smiled upon Mic Wilson at that exact moment. I know I was a huge example of God's people, and I know that somewhere in Heaven a gifted angel was writing such passages as "he sent thy model angel to the dark faces of earth, knowing thy would bringeth much rejoicing by the crushing of God's enemies."

After football practice, my friends all met in the school parking lot deciding what to fill the rest of our after school free time with, sort of passing glances at Kenny, knowing he probably had a hidden stash of marijuana in the glove box of his car.

We knew exactly what we were going to do, since we did the same thing after practice for the last four years, so it was like Kenneth was delaying the impossible when he finally emitted the already rolled joints tucked neatly in his fat black wallet. We took one vehicle and rolled down the street with the simple objectives of sucking down the happy fumes of this fascinating plant, then watching an already seen movie at my place of employment.

We impatiently waited for the contraband to be finally passed around, oh so wanting to be next, watching the next person inhale the excellent smoke of my favorite type of vegetation. Bradley breathed in the large dose and passed the finely rolled entertainment to me. I stuck the end of the joint to my lips while lighting the charred end, I sucked in as much smoke as possible, feeling the powerful effect that is illegal in America.

I already felt lightheaded almost, as I was floating on air looking at all the lighted fast-food billboards that seemed so much brighter and more pleasing. Even though I stayed in the car I was transported to a land of peace, being amused by the brilliant glow of the passing cars that just seemed to smile at me as I got the fighting urge to laugh and dance. I didn't though, I knew I had to keep the calm frame of mind just in case troubles arose.

When we reached the Cinemax I had just finished off a number of drags of this terrific vegetated peacemaker. We went through the back door and quickly found a seat with the paranoid mental state that pot brings you, making you think that everyone coming in contact with you is some kind of police officer. I watched the familiar film that I once hated now convincing myself that this was the greatest performance of all time. The characters were presented with so much color and continued to jump out of the movie screen almost touching me. The actresses seemed so much prettier and they spoke out in a sweet calming voice that only God used.

I looked at Bradley sitting next to me and watched him pay attention to his right hand, as it opened then closed like it was some kind of mechanical device. Jason looked like he was talking to someone as he moved his lips but no sound came out. The customers sitting behind us were probably paying more attention to the strange boys in the front row then what was happening in the film, it was probably the weed thinking for me, but I was sure that someone would be complaining about the bizarre behavior we brought.

After the film, my friends dropped me off at the school to pick up my car. I stood there in the parking lot for a good two minutes before I remembered what I was doing at my most hated location in this great land. I don't know if anyone passed me or walked by during this sleep-like state of daydreaming, but I caused no damage or harm staring at the spectacular grooves of the black pavement. It was dark out, but daytime for me, as I looked for the only car in the school parking lot.

I finally located my car, but another problem was brought to my attention when I lost my keys. I searched in my pockets and looked in places that I would never look when fully sober. I searched underneath my vehicle, thinking maybe I dropped them getting out sometime during the day, not finding them there I then started to backtrack all of my steps that led me to the place I was standing now. I probably was so stoned I may have just walked twice as far as I did to find my vehicle and didn't even realize it. Still, the state I was in brought me joy as I stood there wondering where my keys were when I started to itch the top of my head feeling a surface that was much harder than my fingers. I glanced into the palm of my hand and found the lost items that kept me from returning home.

I walked back to my car happy when I should have

been angry losing my keys once again, but only for about a second quickly remembering where I lost them last time. I slid the keys out of my hand then into my car door now noticing that my transportation was already unlocked and also in gear, trying to remember if I slid into the driver's seat seconds before without knowing it, but it didn't matter since I was now in control and driving down the road.

I was trying to be extra cautious, gripping the wheel with both hands, as I squinted my red eyes for better sight. I remember telling myself getting home in one piece was a simple task, but I can't remember if I was weaving off the road when I felt going over a huge bump, as the car jumped and then bottomed out. I didn't bother to look at what or who I hit, but I didn't really care. I regained control of the car and reminded myself that I was on the simple mission of returning home.

When I got home my father was asleep, while my mother was watching some old rerun on television. She was upset with me not because of how late I returned home, since it was barely 11:30, she just hated me coming home from school at the same late time for the past four years. I remember her asking me what I did that day, as I tried to come up with lies generated from my intoxicated brain, and when she was about to say something else I simply replied, "Nothing."

Steven's Chapter

Dear Diary,

It has been over a week since I have been to school. Every day I walk towards my bus stop until I reach out of my parent's view and then hide behind a tree. I hate school so much and even though I know I must go back, I can't bring myself to show my face. I have been the punch line of all jokes, but never again will I be laughed at. No one will help me and no one accepts me. I am a freak of society and there is not a single person in my school that will recognize my humanity. Please help me Lord, for I have kept your commandments, but my life continues to lead nowhere. I realize Mic is my brother and deep down inside he is a good person, but he continues to allow himself to sin, which is what I think is what causes the anger that he can't control. He always lets it out on me, but why can't he be happy?

No one can be that angry, and why would the Lord allow me to suffer this much. I am nothing. How can I give in to my temptations so easily, I am a pathetic excuse for a Christian. I love you God and I want you to forgive me for what I am about to do. I cannot live the rest of my life like this, so this Friday I will attend school with my dad's 9mm to end all of my torment.

Waking up, I knew today would be the first day of a new life. I looked at my shaking hands and tried to focus them still, but nothing would help. Life felt as a darkened madness, I could of swore all the lighting was purposely dimmed down by some supernatural force, in order to stimulate a more so blackened gloom, for an undeserving freak like me.

I heard my mother calling for me, "Steven breakfast is ready."

With my stomach feeling nauseous from being so nervous, I couldn't possibly eat. I yelled back, "I'm sorry, my stomach feels too queasy for me to eat, but thank you anyway." I felt bad hurting my mother's feelings by declining her tasty meal. She has been so good to me and I know that after today mom is going to have much more to hurt about than her son's malnutrition.

I reached for my clothes and observed the black shiny pistol that lay on the corner of where my clothes sat. Putting on my clothes I pondered my twisted plans, feeling sicker with the mental visuals of what I was about to do. I hated myself for what I have narrowed my life down to, but it constantly felt like there was no other alternatives no matter how sick, I immediately kneeled in prayer for the Lord.

"Jesus forgive me for what I am about to do. I have tried everything and you know I have obeyed you, but there is no way out. Lord bless my mom, I love her so much, I always believed I would give her a better life. Bless my father Lord, please give him a better job. Bless my brothers and sisters, I am lucky to have such great siblings, they don't deserve a freak like myself for a brother. Please feed my three cats and dog Jesus. Again, please forgive me Lord. Amen."

I stood up, grabbed the gun, put it in my bag, and went to the bathroom where I stared at the mirror displaying a sinful disgusting monster that once represented one of the Lord's people.

I began to think of every outrageous unthought of reaction to my plan. Brushing my teeth, I felt my stomach get sick with an even more nauseous feeling. I couldn't hold it; I bent over and vomited the contents of my stomach. I continued to throw up when my mother interrupted my moans.

"Steven, are you ok?"

Of course, like anyone, I replied, "Yeah, I'm ok. I think I might of woke up to fast or something, I'm sure I'll feel fine once I'm at school." But I wasn't fine. Today was both the day all of my pain would end and the day I would force pain in the hearts of everybody else. I knew what I was going to do, but didn't know how I was going to do it. Quickly, I bowed my head and asked for forgiveness.

I looked up, took a deep breath, opened the door, and started for my front door. I felt the steps of my mom behind me, but I just ignored her and continued in my direction.

"You leaving already?"

I felt a little better this time not having to lie to my mom again. "Yeah, I thought I would ride my bicycle to school today," as I progressed on with her back to me.

"Well, come give your mother a hug before you go."

I turned and hugged her tightly, as she gave me her motivational morning speech, she used to say every day.

"Steven, I love you and I want you to do your best."

"I love you too, mom."

"Just do your best and obey your Lord, and you'll make me proud. You always do."

I almost cried in her arms, when she told me how proud I made her, thinking just how proud she would be by the end of the day. How could I do this to her? If only she knew my torment then maybe she would understand, but that didn't prevent all my sadness. Deep down I truly realized all this misery and depression is of my creation, I am such a poor weak-minded fool. I thought that if only I could keep the tears in until I left, mother would not be more suspicious than she already is.

I released my mom and quickly left out the front door. I burst into tears, but still continued to the backyard finding my bike, stood up on the side of my house, all rusting away from the weather. I don't deserve a bike like this; it has lasted with me since my eleventh birthday. I remember how my parents gave me the expensive gift with a huge smile on their faces even though they knew the gift probably meant that my father would have to deprive himself of lunch for the next three or four months. I wiped my tears away, jumped on my old friend, and began to pedal away.

The ride to school was the longest drive in my entire life. The sky beat me down with its lack of sunlight the world seemed dead for some reason. There weren't as many cars out as usual, I felt all alone on this planet and everything was quiet, I knew if I had just listened closely for a moment I could hear the world criticizing me on how low I was. Thoughts filled my head through the whole route, and the feeling of throwing up came again, but there was nothing in my stomach for my mouth to vomit. I was not happy with what I was going to do, but how could I go to school

35

with all my horrible shame, knowing Mic's strange hatred for me will someday again rise. I couldn't take it.

About an hour later I pedaled into the parking lot and then to the bike rack. I set my bike up, as a group of girls passed me yelling out, "Now we know why the guys call you scrawny."

I ignored them, with my sick plans I could hardly hear them. I walked into the gym, listening to some guys yell out, "How'd you like your little early lunch last Friday, ha ha."

School hadn't even begun, but everyone was talking to everyone else in their little trends and groups. I scanned the groups for Mic, when people again insulted and mocked me saying, "You came to school?" Ignoring them, I focused on myself and tried to control my heavy breathing. I began wiping off the beads of sweat running down my face, when I froze to a shrieking alarm that went off in my head.

There he was, standing with all his friends, staring in my direction and laughing, not realizing what was about to happen. I calmed myself down again, reached into my bag and held the black maker of peace in my hand. I hadn't pulled it out yet I just held onto it while it was still in my bag, silently praying to my Lord, then wiping away the tears that sprung from eyes, probably dark pulsing red. I started to walk in Mic's direction, saying to myself I could still back out and try my best to attend high school with all my disrespect. I began walking faster with all of my sin attacking my head, reminding myself I didn't have to go on with my actions, as I watched Mic turn and scream out, "Freak, I like you better not attending school, freak."

Life and all its great gifts of sound slowed and shut off as I pulled out the gun that was in the backpack, pointed it at Mic's head, and pulled the trigger. My heart skipped, but I continued to shoot the dead body of Mic Wilson as it was still standing erect, but then falling. His body was sinking when a bullet passed through him again and then his body laid on the ground lifeless, yet I failed to stop shooting him. Tears poured out of my eyes, as I listened to horrible screams of others, crying for their humble and kind leader. Bullets were still piercing through the air when someone jumped on my back, heavily breathing and screaming in my right ear, trying their best to reach my gun. Without even thinking I immediately pointed the gun over my right shoulder and pulled the trigger. One moment I felt my attackers heart beat to the same continuous rhythm but then totally halt, just as I felt his body warmth, but then it wasn't there, my attacker was dead.

I looked back to see the sight of my teacher's falling body hitting the ground without any attempts to catch himself. I looked up catching everyone's horrified looks, as I collapsed to the ground with sorrow, bawling over my teacher's death quietly crying out, "I'm so sorry." He didn't deserve this, this is not how it was supposed to be, this was totally an accident. I kneeled over my teacher's body, not realizing my actions, but I didn't care. I started to pray, almost out loud, but quiet enough for most not to hear me.

"Forgive me Jesus, I have sinned. Please help me, I am sick, I am a horrible person. I love you. I am so sorry. Please help."

I woke up in a driving police car, listening to two cops continually say, "How could you do it?" The cop on the right looked back at me with red angry eyes and said, "You're in a lot of trouble tough guy." I lowered my head and started to cry, feeling the nasty pain on the back of my head, which was presently bleeding from a blow from a more better person than me. I could do nothing but cry and repent in my sorrows, then hearing one of the cops mumble, "I say we drive the freak out of town and beat him until he can't walk. Show him how tough he really is."

How could this happen? I have always tried to obey the Lord, so why do I have to suffer again. I will not suffer even longer, probably for the rest of my life. I deserve it, they were both good people and no one will ever be able to experience their company again. I am so weak and selfish. How could anyone do such a deed. I was given such a great life and now I show my pathetic thanks by taking the lives of two friends. What a pathetic Christian I am. I am nothing. I wish I were nothing.

"Lord forgive me."

Dear Diary,

This is when I woke up that morning. I burst into tears, and immediately began to repent. Thank God it was just a dream. I had no idea what that dream meant. As I sit here staring at my father's pistol, I remember back, how my head was covered in filth. How my presence was made a mockery and how it will be made fun of again in the future. I held the gun, but only for a second. I got up, got dressed, ate my mother's breakfast, and gave her a huge hug. I told her I loved her and I would make her proud. When she wasn't looking I went into her room and placed my father's gun back in its hiding spot. Then I went to school.

Football, Parties, and Alcohol

Everyday finished with the same basic routine excluding today. Today was the first game day and I focused on nothing but winning, except first I had to scavenge some alcohol for the after game party. My friend, Brad, and I skipped first period to pursue elimination of the frustrating problem of purchasing beer. It usually never served a problem and didn't this time as well. People that purchased us beer were usually mature nerds with nothing to do, and the simple act of contributing to minors probably makes them feel like the winners they never were. After about two calls to some of the pathetic but useful of-age buyers, one person agreed that purchasing me beer was the only way he would ever be hip. Beer now served no obstacle to me and let me focus on greater events such as ignoring school to concentrate on the upcoming game.

I finished school suffering even more through a bit of useless knowledge, as I savagely zoned out the real world to prepare myself for the upcoming football game. I always paid less attention to my schooling on game days, as I determined to set myself in the victorious frame of mind that eliminated any motivation to learn and focused my spirit on winning.

I played quarterback since I was born, and people did not say other than I was the most essential ingredient for my team. I have had Scouts try to convince me to play for their colleges since I was a sophomore, and truly believed that my outstanding arts of football was going to support my future life. Just like being strong, good-looking, and the best talent for throwing came really natural to me, as if I came to this world with a football in my right arm. Still, this was the school's first game and people counted on my great football expertise to win, but everyone needs help sometimes especially when my fellow students would bet their pointless lives on my fantastic skills.

I am guessing that around the middle of the week my band of associates all pitched money in for three boxes of laxatives. The helpful medication originally resembled round yellow pills, but were now smashed into fine powder and placed into clear plastic sand-wich bags. Our foolish contenders arrived to our school a few hours early to practice their plays, mak-ing sure their team was ultimately unstoppable.

Hours before the game, I sent one of my friends over to their sidelines, telling him to fashion himself in a subtle act of flirtation, so the few school spirited that were present saw my buddy as a normal horny high school student. When he did so, he communicated with some of the out-of-town girls to seem like he was just trying to get a long distant relationship, and after a few minutes of his silly flirting he casually inched himself over to the other team's water coolers. When no one was looking, he emptied the crushed deposits out into the coolers swift as possible, trying his best in being concealed.

After completing his job he reported back to me and explained the far-fetched story that I have just fin-ished. Barely believing him, I told him he did well, both of us knowing I would gladly beat him down if he was lying.

We all put on our football equipment that matched our school colors red and black, waiting for our cue to run out on the field, then starting warm ups. All you could hear was the motivating sounds of heavy metal being played on the Varsity's intercom, and singing along were the savage screams of high school patriots now transformed into powerful destroying animals. When it was time to run out on the field the coach always made us sit on one knee to bind all of us in a small prayer. He always started off with a sentimental opening simply asking God to help us but always ended the prayer a little inappropriately, usually saying something like "let us destroy our opponents." I thought it was the perfect way to motivate the team as we then said, "amen" and started to direct ourselves to the door then towards the illuminated football field. All of us made our way through the black background that night delivered, and onto the flood-lit field that always provided a sense of confident belonging. There is something magical about running onto a lit football field listening to a band play the school's theme song while hearing all your friends cheer for you. The spectators continued to cheer on as we all ran to our desired warm-up areas and did all our exercises synchronized while chanting our school name. Like boot camp, this readied ourselves for battle and determined the mind transformation to allow us in crushing without mercy.

Our adversary team was located on the opposite side of the field doing similar warm-ups, not thinking they traveled such a distance to fail, then mourn about the game during the long trip home. Only to arrive in front of all their family and friends, sadly explaining who's fault it was.

I saw hundreds of students yelling out my name in a rejoicing applause, as they put all of their faith in my athletic gifts. After warm-ups we all circled around our father-like coach, and listened to his speech that would provide others with the little amount of confidence that would help my in-game-bodyguards function properly. If only others knew how to speak the same politically correct language, as the coach told us to perform like a team, truly meaning to cover me, so I can comfortably throw touchdown passes.

After the speech, we all ran to our side of the field where sat a huge set of silver metal bleachers containing hundreds of wild fans. I spotted my girl, whose reputation was fastly growing, sandwiched in between two well-known females all three of them blowing me kisses. I recognized my favorite waitress Michelle about two rows up from Jennifer. She sat with a huge group of people all yelling in honor of me, but the only one I brought myself to care about was the slender brunette that smiled. She surprised me for a moment when she ignored her shy personality and opened her legs as an invitation; slightly revealing what was on the other side of her short jean cutoffs. I looked over a couple of rows and observed my friendly jackal who grinned the same time as I, both of us knowing the sweet deed that would help us in victory. Behind my sneaky hitman stood a group of tight shorts that held up a red poster advertising my name and football number in black bold letters. Next to them sat Kenny and Travis both foolishly screaming out my name while pointing in my direction. I had over two hundred fans cheering for me during every game, knowing God would be happy to see how hundreds of followers came to exalt his elite in the respected way they were supposed to. Looking at my adoring fans, I waved them down for a period of silence as they quietly obeyed in preparation for the nation's theme song.

The announcer broke the huge wall of cold silence, as he gave a lovely female singer a small stepping stone in her future. She walked out on the field carrying a black microphone and wearing a suitable dress that probably expressed her singing dream.

As the glare of the floodlights wore off, I began to recognize that the elegant singing performer once called me boyfriend. She was very attractive and I gave no complaints on the way she presented herself but unfortunately, she believed that women served greater and other purposes then nursing to my sexual urges. I'm not saying this singer did not enjoy the memorable gifts that I gave her, because there is no possible way she could not. I just tend to believe that she had other useless plans for life and entertainment that went nowhere after experiencing the riotous road to life then dispensing it, as she chose not giving it up for me.

After the nation's theme she left the applauding sacred field, as it was immediately swarmed with the true reason hundreds of fans crowded the bleachers, to watch the insulting destruction of one school's respect.

Winning the coin toss, the coach decided to receive the ball properly choosing the correct decision, watching the receiver amazingly dart from one side of the war grounds all the way over to the opposite side already establishing the lead. The crowd went berserk as I humorously noticed a few of our opposing players already clenched their stomachs thinking of the closest route to a nearby toilet. I admitted this lucky touchdown was due to the laxatives but didn't expect my biological warfare to already take affect. I caught a couple of foreign football players rush back to the locker rooms as I realized that feeling the humiliation of defeat was impossible for my team.

It was only an hour into the game when our coach started to play never before tested fourth string players that still simply managed to catch my strong passes, making the score sixty-two then sixty-nine then seventy-six. The most pathetic play in the history of football happened during this game when we blitzed our sick enemies. With some quick but foolish thinking they felt that running the ball would change the silly outcome, forcing me to stick on their secret weapon eventually knocking him straight to the ground as if I was hitting some type of defenseless toddler looking back up at his disciplinary figure. There is something extremely wonderful about colliding with a rival which such a force he can't get up. Even more so, as the running back rolled over on the ground with pain and I noticed a brown stain that squirted out, soaking all the way through his pants. The downed fighter with his disgusting uncontrollable bathroom problems fulfilled an act that was easily compared to burning the United States flag. The hilarious situation of our nauseated enemies called another time-out as one of the players retreated off the front lines explaining to his embarrassed coach, he had to make another restroom stop.

Their coach was balancing on the line of crying and killing, looking at all of his once-admired boys, wanting to live the life of any other individual on the planet.

Our coach was understandably acting the exact opposite, bragging at the great football team he trained almost expecting, but not wanting, to admit the strange sickness the other side was suffering through, to give our team the advantage.

I couldn't help to laugh, as our enemies disappeared one-by-one stepping off the sidelines and toward the bathrooms. People started to stare in my direction not knowing what I found so amusing about the situation, so much wishing I could tell someone of my well worked plan. The other team was now players short of being able to stay in the game, so with a smart call of leadership our opponents lowered their heads in shame and forfeited the game.

We won the game seventy-six to zero. I remember never seeing our coach so happy, as he went out of his way to give me a respected handshake. The crowds filled the entire field with loud applause, as I caught a small glimpse of Jennifer, who started to walk in my direction. She started bending over the safety rail that outlined the top of the bleachers and began to softly whisper in my ear.

I hope she didn't expect me to cherish the sweet expression "you're my hero" because what she would give me tonight at the party would definitely act as a bigger sentimental piece. After the feeling of being her hero she gently kissed me on the lips and told me she would later meet me at the party. Not too early of course, I had plans with a young brown-haired waitress that promised me she would be coming to see me, knowing she might as well show up wearing no pants and we would both save a lot of time.

As Jennifer started to leave, my racing thoughts for her were interrupted by the attractive friends advertising my name with the huge red poster. They fought their way just close enough so I could hear them ask a huge share of questions about my later celebration of underaged drinking. As I replied back more than ecstatic to invite these model examples of envious women. As my sweet looking fans departed they were only to be replaced by another asking questions of the legendary after-game party that took place at my home.

Most of the party animals that showed up befriended me in no way, but everyone had a part in my sexual goals by spreading the word or bringing a bunch of intoxicated females that couldn't wait long enough to drink at the party. I care a lot about different roles in life in fact I could be just as happy with the great feeling of alcohol coursing through my system, but doing any activities while drunk is just a lot more amusing.

I told a huge number of useless people of the party when I luckily spotted a more than worthy person to invite. I quickly finished my sentence with the current alcohol-deprived teenager and started to walk towards the area where Michelle clung to the safety rail. I could not remember the outfit Michelle was wearing, but that wasn't important, after consuming a couple of beers this nice girl wouldn't be wearing anything at all.

With her hand still on the rail I reached out and softly touched it. She immediately jerked around and glared at me with a pair of surprising eyes, as she excitedly started to speak of my expertise towards football. She won the short contest of flattering me, probably her style of making sure she was still invited to my party, but I determined she made attendance at my social gathering with or without her sweet remarks.

After explaining that her company would be greatly appreciated at my huge niche, I slipped off to the locker rooms answering no more questions from anyone else. Since conversing with Michelle in the guarantee that plans of my drinking festival was the only reason I was still mingling to others.

When I walked in the locker room, there was a huge commotion of celebrated laughter, as teammates started to pat me on the back and yell out "there's the real hero of the game." I am glad that the real hero was not mistaken for the coach or some other undeserving fool who probably scored the only touchdown he will ever make unless of course I pull off another food poisoning act.

I tried to change my sweat-drenched uniform as fast as I could only to begin drinking and host my party. I stripped off my clothing and joined all of my fellow winners in the steaming shower room witnessing but not witnessing everything the female students dreamed about.

The size of a man's genitalia also served a factor in popularity mostly with the males, knowing I was blessed being larger then most, I never had to focus my worries in this area. It is one of man's most cherished parts of the body and anyone born abnormally small was made fun of by the other guys, branding the poor man with a silly nickname that usually stayed with him the rest of his high school life. Being born as big as I was, I used my trait as a heroic weapon of art. If my penis had a personality it would mostly resemble the Mona Lisa making me Leonardo Da Vinci creating some of the greatest masterpieces in the world. If my imagination could best describe my splendid art piece it would probably look like a long reflective sword being thrust up into others, except in the realistic world man's mate truly want my sword pounded into them as if I was actually going to battle.

After making myself presentable, I quickly transported myself back to my gigantic cottage all while consuming a couple of beers on the way, aware the quicker I drank the faster the excellent sensation of alcohol would fulfill its job throughout my body.

After finishing off three cans of my favorite beverage I arrived at my miniature mansion, only to be visited by a few impatient drinkers who were parked in my driveway making themselves at home just waiting for the eloquent party to begin. To my great and fortunate surprise among my waiting party animals turned out to be the very attractive server Michelle, leading a huge band of friends that followed her in pairs, as two blondes chased after, and then two horny guys probably filling there minds in excitements of getting lucky. I immediately invited them in, while presenting them all with a beer and providing one for me. I accomplished my first objective when I felt the beer taking affect in my body, so I began my second goal in short time all by starting off with flattering Michelle with sweet expressions that she, with no question, wanted to hear.

We all directed ourselves in the basement to play a game of pool and dance to the funky sounds of my state-of-the-art stereo system, which was also hooked up to the television set but sat unused in such huge celebrations where there was much more pleasing entertainment. My basement was the perfect location to socialize in such events because it was untouched by the dull desires of the adult's mind, allowing me the advantage of installing tools like a black light and also a strobe light.

My human creators hardly ever went down there so I took the liberty of tacking up insulting pictures but praising portraits of woman that hung on walls painted a spaced out shade of blue and purple. I also painted eerie neon designs on some of the basement walls that third dimensionally jumped out due to the black light and the contribution of beer influencing my body with the smallest bumbling extreme. After a couple of beers I sat down on my couch to rest, when I started to notice others were getting just as drunk as I, listening to the abnormal amount of laughter that was going on. The unwritten law of not touching the opposite sex was also being broke, watching Michelle stumble near, then stand way too close to me for a sober person.

Alcohol was also a truth serum it forced individuals to act the way they truly felt and wanted. I don't know if she was going to ask me a question as she faced me at an elevated height, but before she did I wrapped my arms around her so my head was resting on her stomach. After a moment she turned away and sat on my lap as I again wrapped my arms around her giving her the sensation of being special.

When drinking, it takes a small effort for even the perfect stranger to make you feel like someone special and it also takes the corniest joke to make you laugh. I loved alcohol and the founders of this magnificent drink should be congratulated, for only a mastermind could invent a liquid that could make one's body perform in such a way. The ingredient of this splendid drink was in no doubt a gift from God, given to us for the use of leisure time and the strenuous passing of a long stressful day. It made those who would normally never speak to each other best friends for the night and gave one a large amount of confidence. The drug made women a lot prettier and left those who drink heavily in unexplainable situations like waking up in places you have never seen before. I watched the drug work on Michelle as she stood up then started to dance by herself, and with the beer thinking for me I then convinced myself she was one of the most charming girls I have ever seen.

People started to show up by the packs, some already drunk only waiting to join in the great festivities such as dancing, socializing, and me. After people started to show up I nominated friends to inform others to park in the correct location, while another buddy was given the job of opening the door to the freshly arriving, this let me flirt with Michelle who was now well on her way of getting drunk.

I took a short recess from Michelle to introduce myself to the other females that showed up and after telling a couple of jokes, I noticed a small act of betrayal. I observed some without a beer and tried to offer them one, but with the poor excuse of being the designated driver, they declined. I believe the fear of drunk driving is a tale made up to scare others since I have had countless experiences in this silly issue and lived to tell about it almost every single weekend. I have always used high vainness for these party traitors who constantly used the dumb recycled excuse of not drinking mostly because they probably grew too fond of their parental figures who brainwashed into their minds the ridiculous saying that drinking was bad. I was always curious to see what exactly these drinkless folk were doing in such an alcohol-infested area.

Somewhere in America there are government officials who waste their time on wars and political issues, but when they understand the greater pleasures in life, I hope they find it in their hearts to create my perfect law: whosoever shows up at such a huge celebration may not leave the very grounds until he or she cannot walk due to the drugs in that person's system.

Even though I found these dishonorable party animals very disturbing I wasn't about to let the paranoid put a stop in my fun. The seven beers I had already consumed were doing a great job in entertaining me. I was about to stumble my way over to some of my associates, who were also influenced by the alcohol, but with the music thumping out in a catchy beat I was grabbed by the arm surprised by a very intoxicated version of Michelle. I then grabbed her around the waist pulling her close enough for her to feel what I would later give her. I was having the most enjoyable time with Michelle, under strobe lights dancing among the rest of the swingers. Both of us trying our best not to bump into others, as we moved in the most dirtiest and outlawed form of dancing, grabbing each other everywhere except for appropriate portions of our bodies.

It was probably safe to say Michelle probably had about five beers too many when she jumped on me wrapping her legs around my body. I began kissing her, as we both tried to keep with the beat while still going at each other orally. The thrilling situation was not a first time for me but I enjoyed it tremendously, knowing I still had to perform on these great curves before my girlfriend arrived. With the alcohol and the little amount of light no one could truthfully describe what we were doing so rumors of cheating on Jennifer didn't really bother me.

I had enough of all this clothed intimacy, and I couldn't get the full feeling in such a crowd, so after about four songs of showing our affection towards each other I put her down off my body, then slightly suggested resting upstairs for awhile.

I watched the tight jeans try her best to stand correctly, as I led Michelle up the stairs, and could obviously see she had no idea where I was bringing her. I walked her down the hall and to my room, filling with excitement, knowing that the ending of the day could have been fun or it could have been extremely exhilarating, but watching Michelle in her drunken state I knew my night would be both.

I opened the door of my dark room and laid Michelle down on my bed, immediately kissing her, I unbuttoned her shorts then pulled them down, as she started to rip off the rest of her own clothing. I continued kissing her then licked my way down her neck, she then unzipped my jeans and managed to pull them down slightly. I started to thrust myself between her legs and noticed her actions slowly cease then completely stop. As she started to pass out I did what any other caring human would do and tried to wake her up by pounding myself inside her.

This entertaining drunk did not wake up but sometimes it's better this way, since I got what I desired and she won't remember me giving her something extremely wonderful. Therefore I won't have to deal with breaking another heart in telling her I would rather have Jennifer.

After I was done, I gently slipped her clothes back

on to give the impression that this girl did nothing else but pass out in my bed. Just for the sake that Jennifer will also come over and not be angry at me for easing my sexual addiction on someone else. I threw a blanket over her and returned downstairs to the party only to find the head count was multiplied by two.

It's funny how the greater points in life are all witnessed in a slow enough motion to gradually stop. The sight I was currently witnessing was so beautiful I could have painted the elegant scenario and sold it with a priceless dollar sign to some art gallery, standing right next to the Mona Lisa. Not that I cared for the Mona Lisa, it would be more like the Mona Lisa standing next to my outstanding masterpiece, and my artwork would be the inspiration of millions, trapped inside of dozens of big security officials. If I could convince the Almighty to halt time long enough for me to create, I would paint the fine sight of underage drinkers sitting around my coffee table sipping on the delicious liquid of hard liquor. I would paint the huge majority trying their best in dancing while the fantastic drug forced strangers to touch other strangers in the most sacred parts of the human body. I would even paint the people who choose to stay sober, which even though I hated, these people showed up at every party. I would paint my favorite companions telling sick jokes that only we understood and drinking beers all while playing a game of pool that determined a different champion with the perfectly matched skills my chaps had. I would even add in the anti-social group that sat in the corner of the room which I rated higher than some since they all had some type of splendid alcoholic beverage in their hand. My masterpiece would grow to infinite lengths in every aspect especially showing the evil what God's people did on their leisure time.

When I walked in everyone presented me with a greeting, as they all replied out "Mic" in a synchronized joyous yell, then shutting off the music, as most of them asked me to recite a speech in honor of throwing the school's first party. Everyone was now so intoxicated I could have said anything at all and they would have all cheered like I was in some kind of queer pageant answering a question about the environment.

It was funny to see people reduced in such ways and watch the alcohol give certain individuals enough confidence in doing things they would normally never do, but when they all started to forget why they were silent, I spoke. I told them I was glad they all could make it to my party and repeated a serious speech once told by a character on a television program, now making it a humorous motivating inside joke, since they were also all raised by the same television and knew of the same speeches.

After humorously applauding for my words they turned up the music, then started off finishing the movements they stopped in, and I headed straight for the brown coffee table that stood three different bottles of hard liquor. The coffee table sat in front of a dark blue couch, which was used to sit people watching television, but today it sat a maxed out amount of abusive drinkers playing drinking games with vodka. I could feel the influence of alcohol slowly wearing off my body, so I had no choice but to join in on this familiar game of gambling away your sober state of mind.

This particular game was played with a cup and one quarter. You tried to bounce the quarter off the table and land it into the cup that was filled with liquor.

A person making a direct shot gets to shoot again and chooses another to drink the contents in the cup. After making it three times in a row that person develops a rule, which usually forced the drunkest female to take off an article of clothing every time anyone else had to drink.

There were six of us playing and with me being the newest player, I went first. For a little comic relief, I stalled a bit trying to see how long I could mumble on, forcing one of the impatient to lash out and tell me to begin. My little inside joke went on for so long all the waiting contestants screamed out at the same time, then watched me like a hawk when I finally pursued to take my gamble. With the uncomfortable stare of others it seemed as though time slowed down, as I lifted the silver coin and bounced it off the brown surface of my coffee table. The quarter spun around then went straight into the cup disrupting the calm surface of this clear liquid in a tiny splash. There were only two girls playing, but I could definitely tell one did not share the sober status with the other, so I thought it would only be fair if this thirsty female received a little taste of alcohol in her system.

I pushed the cup in her direction, as she glanced at me for a second then pouted like she truly didn't crave the drink. She lifted up the short term housing of this gracious liquid then brought the glass to her mouth downing the contents with a cringed look on her face the strong taste liquor brought. We all laughed at her as I took my turn again but missed my target by a couple of inches.

After finishing off two bottles of this drug I looked up and started to notice that some of my fellow drunks were getting a little too wild in their alcohol guided dance steps. I didn't think much of it, so I resumed back into the game, when the girl across from me pushed the cup towards myself in explanation that I was the next to drink in her revengeful winnings. I lifted the glass to my mouth and gulped down this small dose of drinker's juice. The burning sensation was the only aspect I was concentrating on at the moment, then when I began to place the cup down one of the intoxicated dancers tripped on his own feet landing directly in the middle of my coffee table, spilling all of the remaining liquor on the carpet, bringing the game to a halt. Everyone playing stood up immediately trying to evacuate from the commotion, with thought of Vodka stained into their clothing.

People started to fixate themselves at what just happened, as I helped this example of clumsiness to his feet, then walked him over to my bathroom leaving the alcoholic overacting fool to cause all the trouble he desired in an adult version of time out. I told him to stop acting like a moron and asked some people to make sure that he did nothing except station himself inside the bathroom. I cleaned up the mess as people started to ask me questions even though they probably wouldn't be able to understand watching how much they strained to stand in one place.

I don't care how drunk anyone is, fulfilling mistakes like this is totally inappropriate and is also a huge party foul that marks a person as a threat in inviting to future parties. I have never acted in such a way when not sober, even at the present moment I observed the world as it bobbed in all directions, and still proceeded to act civilized. I never lost control or embarrassed myself in front of others, showing I couldn't hold my liquor, if I desired I could outdrink anyone at this party and still have enough energy to win some type of iron man contest.

After explaining what happened to a few, someone told me that the overacting drunk escaped from his white bathroom cage, but I thought I might give him a second chance in acting human. So, I just watched him when he just began to walk past me in a stumbling fashion. He headed for the huge crowd of dancers, starting to dance his way towards a female who was alone and also noticing the pathetic drunk in uncomfortable glances. He then started to put his arm around the girl when she jumped back in disgust and fled to the other side of the crowd, hoping to send this under-the-influence fool the impression that she would rather dance with any other person alive than with this bumbling drunk. When the lady dancer left him in insult he paused in question for only a second then started again to the best of his intentions towards dancing, as he bumped and shoved himself into the surrounding couples almost knocking them to the ground. Bradley and I grabbed him by the arms carrying him towards the couch, as I explained the reason for calming down. The drunk then broke free and pushed me back first into the nearest wall, screaming out vain words of vulgar hostility. He then backed up to swing a punch at me when Bradley wrapped his arm around his neck from behind, and started to pull back. I then quickly picked up his feet, while we both shuffled our way to the front door, leading outside.

Everyone was now watching as Bradley and I lifted this insulting party animal out the front door, then with a couple of sways we heaved him onto my front lawn. He got up and again started with his vulgar speech, as he walked towards me in a violent fighting threat. I waited for the moment then kicked this walking party stopper directly in the face, knocking him to the ground, as he began to quietly moan, while grasping his bloody face. With the alcohol still influencing his body the pain didn't bother him enough to realize that no one shared compassion for his injury, that was totally at his fault. He then stood up, as I pushed him down again returning the fool to the place where he stood up. When it looked like he chose a perfect area to pass out for the long cool night this bumbling stubbornness, surprisingly stood to his feet only to flee in the opposite direction. He ran down the dark street probably with plans of human acceptance, but nobody heard of him until the following school day.

No one enjoys the abusive presence of a filthy drinker who doesn't care to think, especially at a huge social event like this. That is all the reason I allowed him departure, knowing I didn't care if he jumped out in front of a moving truck, but for the sake of my humble reputation I acted like the evacuation of this moron was a horrible event.

I have seen this same scenario happen at a number of occasions, where an individual of the small alcohol tolerance becomes disruptive and sometimes develops absurd ideas that their friends are the ones that mock them. They then start to increase a hatred for those closest to them, finally thinking that acting out on their friends in violent behavior is the correct decision that will stop all heckling, that is truthfully due to their pathetic style of absorbing the spectacular gifts of alcohol. Only the weak and foolish act in these ways even when they have the excuse of alcohol to hide behind.

After answering a couple of questions to the unobservant, I tried to calm everyone down by offering more beer and suggestions of the entertaining arts in dancing.

After this unexpected confrontation, most of the weak-minded departed home in the useless wasted thoughts of what would become of the misunderstood kid who ruined my party. Some people's minds are not developed enough to realize what they sincerely care about and base there feelings on what they learned from so-called role models, leaving them with no choice but to hurry home in strange situations like these.

It was only one in the morning when this peculiar incident of destructive alcoholic behavior unfolded, but by the time of 1:30 my home was left with Bradley, who like me would never let a small detail ruin his fun. Jennifer, and the two girls that sat with her who were all now walking through my front door, asking what happened to the attendance of the party. I then explained the bizarre situation to these girls, almost positive that they would also leave because of the abnormal disappearance of the weak party animal, but I retrieved a beer for my new guests not even asking if they would enjoy a sip. I then watched Jennifer and her pals accept the fact that I was forcing them to get drunk.

I began drinking again, while keeping detail that every female held a beer in their hand at all times, knowing the sooner I got them drunk the easier it would be to get more than just Jennifer to join in on the later acts of perversion. The girls knew I was obviously trying to get them drunk, but down inside these pretty faces came to my house for the simple reason of consuming alcohol beverages. I knew they also arrived for the long chance of bragging to their lady friends that they had the privilege of allowing Mick Wilson have his way with them.

As I flirted with my girl, Bradley found himself very interested in one of Jennifer's friends, but that left one female out feeling lonely and depressed, so I switched on groovy sounds to give the sense of a real party that sent all of us dancing. I still felt bad for these mistreated curves, truly knowing Jennifer wouldn't allow a third player in our ending naked acts of lust, still it was safe to assume that she would be ok, with every beer she drank. I noticed her smooth flowing speech started to slur and her dancing got a little sloppy. I also noticed the same with Jennifer, as I looked through my own watery eyes, that tried to focus on suspending my girlfriend up, all while keeping myself standing also.

After a couple of intoxicating perverted dances with my girl we both decided to sit down and rest from this tiring ritual of affection, when she took me by surprise saying how she would enjoy playing a game of strip poker. Watching Jennifer's friend agree to play this fine game where the jackpot is getting your opponents naked, was also an act due to my favorite drug. Every time alcohol is in perspective I am reminded of why I am so fascinated by the liquid concoction knowing Jennifer would normally never suggest taking off her clothes in front of people she barely knew.

Playing this game before I knew how enlightening watching others gamble there clothes away can be, so without even asking my friend Bradley I automatically assumed that he would be more then happy to join in on this fantastic game.

We all sat around my coffee table, as Bradley was nominated to deal out the cards I sat to the right of Bradley and Bradley's favorite sat to the right of me. Jennifer was straight across from me and to her right sat the pretty girl that no one wanted, probably because she didn't socialize enough.

It is strange how some of the most slender curves will stay untouched because of the lack of talking and this is the very reason that separates me from the lower class. I judge things for their equality and what is right. I don't look at shy girls as an object of untouchable, but for the way she presents herself in a pair of jeans. I don't look at parties as underage disruptive behavior and a way to promote drunk driving; I see parties as a way to socialize with strangers in a different state of mind. Alcohol-related car accidents are not a horrible regretful mistake, but a way to teach others that they were not a good enough driver in the first place. Death by overdosing on drugs and alcohol is not an ignorant mistake, but a way to die while having fun.

Bradley passed out the playing cards, explaining the rules, making sure everyone would take off a piece of clothing when they were really supposed to and not act like they didn't know how to play when they lose, then telling the dealer to start all over again. I lifted up my can of beer to take a small sip, receiving my cards. The hand I was given didn't impress me much, so I gave them back all except for the ace of spades, which I slipped under the table undetected, all credited to the superb effects of alcohol. I was given back a much worthier hand that consisted of three black number cards, another ace, and the wild deuce that we all agreed on, before the game started. I pulled the stolen ace from its small niche and won as I watched the first pieces of clothing being tossed to the floor. When we all handed in the cards to begin the next hand I quickly took advantage of the situation and so humbly kept two of the winning aces back underneath the table for the next set of losing hands.

The losers of this game will not cheat and that's what makes them losers, still I try to not refer to my style of playing poker as cheating. All of the greatest poker players play the game as I do and this is the reason they are so lucky at winning.

After a couple of hands everyone, except for me, was down to the skin tight fabrics of their underwear but every player kept away from being embarrassed with the alcohol still affecting our minds.

We all stared at our cards when I called, as every player started to question my continuous winning touch. The white top half of their underclothes came off as all the ladies tried there best to cover themselves up. Bradley sat motionless hiding behind a table that worked just as well as any pair of briefs, when playing this game. I grunted out sounds of encore, watching my fellow players sit half-naked, staring at me and wondering how I still played the game fully clothed. Bradley dealt out the cards and once again giving me a less then worthy hand to play with, but due to my hidden wild cards, I won with a four of a kind. I watched the feminine bodies strip off their remaining clothes, as I started to again scream out in mocking applause.

I couldn't see the lower portion of their bodies because of the protective covering of my coffee table but I caught glimpses of their mother-like attributes with every movement they made and noticed the walking pleasures that belong to me had the biggest characteristic traits. Jennifer's breasts were perfections of art, slightly hanging, round, and perky, but they had a tint of white that was from the lack of sunshine. Even so, I fought off the sexual urge of just reaching across and squeezing them. The mother-like attributes that belong to the other females were also nice but not as big, still oh how nice it would be to reach over and rub them down, as they currently bounced and swayed, when not covered. With three naked very attractive females displayed before my vision the sexual motives that materialize inside me enhanced increasingly.

With mostly everyone naked, my losing players started to give uninterested movements trying to get at the idea of not wanting to pursue in the game. I looked at Jennifer, as she was trying her best to cover herself up, meanwhile swaying around in a drunken circle motion. With her hands covering herself she started to stand up only to stumble and fall straight on her back, revealing everything she was covering. We all laughed at my drunken girlfriend as she ended the game with her silly mistake of clumsiness.

Somewhere there is an unwritten law that says after playing strip poker a person should look for a place to pass out. This place was usually another's bed, carpet floor, couch, or any surface found suitable, and in Bradley's case, he would be resting in the arms of his lovely stranger, both on top of my bed. I knew where I was going to fulfill my night's rest but first I had a little bit of business to attend to with Jennifer.

I carried Jennifer's drunken body up to my parents' bedroom, as she whispered soft passages that made no sense at all. I pushed open my parents' bedroom door and laid her on top of the bed, gently sitting next to her. She smiled then started to kiss me, as I started to caress the inside of her thighs and said a silent prayer, thanking God for alcohol.

The Popularity Contest

I was told nothing other than "thank you for the amusing party," that following week. I was also given questions of when the next celebration would be taking place. My mother and father decided to dwell at home this weekend so that forced myself to pursue different styles of entertainment.

First I had to find something to do during the scheduled school time of 8:00 A.M. until 1:00 P.M. I felt that I deserved a little spontaneous vacation from the education system that so blindingly taught me close to nothing.

It was Friday and I was spending it with my loyal pals, all of us sitting around my television set being educated in more worthier ways while working off the relaxed sensation of marijuana. It was a fine way of abandoning school even though we had to return at 1:00, we watched television, played pool, and violent video games. We listened to new types of music, conversed with each other, and I began the presentation I had to give at 1:00.

The speech was for the power of my class's presidency, since I again abandoned school last year, not aware I was taking a day off during the presentation date of running for the presidency of the entire school. This civilized popularity contest was a mere waste of time to my rivals, and with the knowledge of all the voters I already claimed all power in the school without the label of serving as a student officer. Finally taking my power seriously, I thought I would find my place as a leader and allow my fellow students to vote for the law and order they have so patiently waited on. Yet, justice did not follow with the name, my voters are lost without me so voting me into a distinguishable source would grant everyone a good realization of where I am. This would issue people the ability of questioning me the inappropriate favors of illegal drugs and alcohol.

It was time to return to school when I found my speech consisted of only three words. My racing mind was still influenced to the state of declining any ideas that could even be considered a rational thought. It didn't matter though, I trusted my popularity would allow me to insult my watching audience and still recognize my destined rights, as class president.

As my friends and I scampered back to my school's lair I confronted what I did best by exploiting my great physical features, as convinced voters sprayed me with adored indications of favoritism. Everyone was aware that I was running for office as they retained out admired actions that their vote was unquestionably mine.

We all routed our direction to the school's gym as the time informed us of a small tardy, which was faulted towards the contraband that has delayed our appearance many times, but it was still not important enough to be cared about. When we entered the enormous building I was greeted by the swelling applause of my senior class, directing myself to the empty white lawn seat, parallel to the chair of my opponents, located in the center of the gym. My friends found seats in brown empty retractable bleachers that sat hundreds of my satisfied voters.

The roar of my fellow students died down, as my grieving principal hid behind a black microphone and began an incoherent dull lecture of being late. He tried to set some type of example out of me by a useless joke that left the audience in an intercepting silence. I was halfway to my seat when my disidolizing principal made a fool of himself and I started to recognize that my brave rival was none other then the insulting creature Steven Parker. I'll admit that this inevitable misery had a vivid courageous mind to quietly sit with belief that he would be voted class president. I slowly sat down and pondered the perfect presentation I had been seeking the past hour, staring at this unbelievably abnormal freak thinking I could open my speech with kicking his dirty face then end with the simple phrase of "vote for me." I sheathed my rabid idea, knowing how inappropriate others would see it as, and watched my lame antagonist immediately counteract to his own name assuming it was his turn to verbally lose.

Even before Steven started to speak my friends hammered his depleted respect with loud humorous insults that veined through the audience in an entertaining trend. Steven now spoke to an enormous army of screaming criticism as I fought off overdeveloped laughter. The rampaging canopy of anarchy was immediately smothered as our egotistical principal claimed back the school in an authority-focused stand followed by a false threat of declining class officers that year. The spotlight was returned to Steven as he stared down hundreds of enemies in puzzlement now realizing, why bother. With a large amount of stubbornness the nerd stepped forward and confronted everyone that hated him, as he nervously began to speak.

"Throughout my life you have all ridiculed and criticized every aspect about me. The only thing I ask of you is to disregard my different not understandable ways and judge me for my highlights. At the present time we are capsized in a place of learning. We wake up every morning and swarm to school in assurance that we make it on time only to learn nothing. I have developed a theory that will allow everyone to learn in a swifter style that is ten times easier. My theory will also eliminate the complex problem of the absent number of teachers, letting sums of money to be used in worthier areas. If I am president motivated students will be given the opportunity to extend their future in computers and work during school hours. Please do not vote against me relying on the weirdo you have stereotyped me as. I am running for class president because I believe I will make a difference, so will you help me build this world?"

Steven baby-stepped back to his chair in dead silence as I stood to attack the microphone with the speech I did not have. I opened my presentation with some comic relief as I unnecessarily cleared my throat for about sixty seconds and when my friends' laughter died down I spoke.

"Don't vote for me. I mean it! Don't vote for me."

I sat back down and watched my reverse psychology work on my school as a humorous accomplishment, witnessing hundreds of school companions shimmer with laughter. Humor was one of the greatest weapons and also another tool of popularity. Being funny was a towering ingredient in making others comfortable, and convincing chicks that the center of attention was reason enough in disposing of the imaginary fable, wait until marriage.

I accepted my throne with a huge wall of laughter that just began to dissipate with a school bell, immediately marking voting hours and the beginning of a new weekend. Now that Steven and I both had a chance to speak, students were given the decision of voting or traveling elsewhere to start their weekend. I quickly departed the boring educational structure to hurry the entertainment that would be found in time, knowing my presence and vote would be trifle unnecessary with the worshiping public that needed me.

Bradley, Kenneth, Travis, and myself all hopped into Bradley's transportation, as the black stereo thumping Bronco ate up the dark road, gladly leaving our school to the voters and the pathetic janitors that will stay to scrub the toilets.

Janitorial occupations are the jobs of freaks that waste their time with activities in connection with computers, books, or the other nameless substitutions of nerdy traits. This degrading job advertises evildoers by the dirty errand of maintaining a clean toilet from human waste, using the hands that feed themselves. Janitors ranked way below all disgracing employment, which also stands with pool men and plumbers. God made it this way to punish wicked people by forcing them to clean for the hip, like my losing hated opponent Steven Parker; he will someday also experience this deserving employment.

Traveling back to my wealthy neighborhood my associates and I all hypothesized the outcomes that will route the remainder of the day, but with our declining imaginations we were left with nothing. As we drove closer to my house we began to pass glances at Kenneth with the assured assumption that the drug dealer would have some kind of worthy drug that would fulfill the passing of a Friday night. There was a long quiet pause of silence, while all of our minds were heading in the same direction of who would be the courageous individual to break this punishing silence and ask our drug dealing companion if he had any concealed paraphernalia of some type.

Patiently waiting for someone to inappropriately question our friend, the drug dealer reached into the right pocket of his jeans. pulling out what looked like an eyedropper. Kenneth untwisted the cap to this puzzling clear bottle, lifted it to his mouth, and dropped a single piece of liquid onto his pink probing tongue. With me planted in the closest horizontal seat as Kenny, the dealer handed me the small plastic bottle urging myself to enjoy the next mind expanding hit of LSD.

We were extremely thankful when the mysterious liquid turned out to be one of the most fantastic achievements in science and every one of us graciously showered our above-the-law companion with thrilling encouragement. The black Bronco pulled onto my long cement driveway when I felt the drop of acid hit my tongue as I again thanked Kenny for not letting us down, then passing the bottle to the nearest person.

That is what I liked about Kenneth, if obvious figures show that a day full of boredom will arise he will always have a backup plan. He is a good man even though the law finds his interesting employment full of injustice and disgust. His under-the-table occupation is very important to hundreds of people and also his closest friends, knowing he will always have some type of untested drug up his sleeve. There is absolutely nothing wrong with Kenny's money-making theories, in fact the single act my associate could be charged with is that he makes others happy. The particular drug that he so generously provided us with was followed by an unexplainable feeling that I ranked towering over marijuana, but a couple of notches below my favorite drug, alcohol.

After the mind-expanding liquid circled the truck three more times we exited Bradley's parked car and entered my abandoned niche, but only for awhile realizing once one of my caring guardians got off work they would return home to a structure full of legally crazing high school stars. We all went down to our reoccurring hangout destination allowing the fantastic drug to take effect of our bodies while we all calculated ideas of where to depart before my parental counterparts arrived back home.

One hour passed when I noticed the couch I rested on began to slowly move in and out as if it was breathing. I watched the good-looking poster woman smile at me, then opened a subject of discussion that explained to myself how peculiar it was that we both have so much in common. The drug made me happy and I displayed it with uncontrollable laughter, springing from an unknown source. I saw my friends giggle as they played a game of pool, with their goals set on hitting multi-colored balls that probably begged them to stop. The pool sticks left long image tracers with ever jolting movement, and the ground was moving in a number of separate swirling vortexes. Sitting beside me was Bradley, waving his car keys in front of his face, while talking directly into the surrounding atmosphere. I could hear and observe enlightening tunes of music sprouting from my stereo system, as I tried my hardest to remember who switched it on. Intercepting the lovely sensation I was enduring, rounded all of my giggling buddies to depart my humble home in avoidance of any interviews with my soon returning parents.

All of my smiling associates piled in Bradley's automobile, as he quickly turned his car on and sped down the house outlined road, in a tiny swerving pattern. He drove ten notches under the speed limit, understandably so, as he accepted a huge amount of responsibility driving in his confusing state. Kenny and Travis glued their eyesight upon the road helping the driver in assurance that our unknown destination would be reached.

I watched the sunlit world change colors from the front passenger seat, when the Bronco traveled on different streets with no collaborated motives of where it was going to end up. I paid no attention to where we were and where we stopped, but in a small amount of time I realized all my companions opened their doors to get out.

With a forceful startling level of focus I noticed that my esteemed friend Bradley navigated our direction towards the local mall establishment. I couldn't think of a greater place to enjoy the enchanting pleasures of LSD without the awkward resistance of a parental guardian.

Parents always continue to establish obstacles in the highway of life's most important activities. They exaggerate everything fun in a sinful way, and pursue their hardest to prevent their children in what they stereotype as everything they once were, unacceptable. They oppose their children's decision of friends and social standards then hypocritically do the deeds they just criticized. My children will have the privilege of freedom in all of their desires and be able to flaunt ideas to all of their friends, while throwing a party with their father present.

The following couple of hours were passed mostly just walking from store to store, while observing every single aspect that usually carries on as unnoticeable, when sober. I saw the mirror-like reflections in every store window, which was supposed to look like me, but declined any resemblance at the present moment. I took time to actually listen in on the pathetic communication that every working clerk had to say, as I fixed my eyesight on faces of strangers that began to twist and distort when they looked back. I purchased some golden French fries, which grew to portray the look of yellow fried worms slithering about begging me not to consume them. I was having a great time.

When we left the mall it was dark out and ready for our next fun filled adventure that was manipulated, while sucking in all of the great swirling patterns of clothing store perfumes. The perfume fragrance lingered outside and like the music, the smells actually had mass, growing out like a gigantic jungle plant. It was almost a week since the villain, and now runner-up in the school institution of politics, Steven Parker received a good beating so plans of showing up in his neighborhood were all I could think of.

I achieved Steven's address years ago from the city's phone book long before his number became unlisted due to my continuously hilarious prank calls. I don't know if my threatening calls are the circumstances that pushed the freak over the edge or if it was the time I transformed his local number into a homosexual dating service, by printing the number on every bathroom stall in the school. Parker changed his home number at a few occasions, until the school stubbornly realized that some of the students were sneaking in other pupils' personal files, after hours. Tormenting Steven on the phone was an extremely cheap extracurricular activity that felt so enjoyable one could achieve an entire day of fun without the usage of drugs.

We all directed our way in a distorted reality towards my right arm's Bronco and entered it, when I calmly suggested my splendid plan for nature's disgust. I lacked an idea at the present moment, but the four of us agreed that the suffering of Mr. Steven was a lovely reason to once again risk our lives in driving Kenny and Travis started up with their anti-car accident method, as I concocted an idea of misery thinking how grand it would be to taste a satisfying beer right about now.

The Bronco was parked about a block away from Steven's poor excuse of a home as the four of us hid, while still under the influence, outside dying bushes that surrounded a filthy white small trailer. The vertical houses were the same in that they demanded a responsible owner that actually cared for the way they presented themselves. A front yard was absent as well as house windows, which were replaced by black plastic and also a dependable transportation vehicle. A truck was parked in front of a cement block that was used as a doorstep and his truck had chips of paint peeling off dented steel. The vehicle probably ceased to start anyways observing an old dirty car engine covered in grass that was placed on the side of his trailer.

Next to the engine sat a grease-infested red push lawnmower, which sat as an antique in the present time, knowing all that was left in the front yard were some bushes and rocks. There was about three cats nested in different places of his land, one directly on the hood of his pathetic car and two near the leaning mailbox that was closer to where we stayed camou-flaged.

Bradley also noticed this then looked at me and with both of our mental abilities working at a similar rate I snatched one, while he grabbed the other. We cradled the cats in our arms while swiftly running back to the Bronco, trying our best not to reveal the laughter that would find us trouble. Once Kenny and Travis saw us frantically scamper off they quickly fol-lowed knowing a great idea was about to unfold. We threw the furry pets inside the Bronco as we all jumped in and sped off driving at a huge accelerated speed. The Bronco pursued off in the opposite direc-tion of Steven's home as a terrific suggestion sprouted in my mind that dealt with the ornery black cat, I forced calm in my lap.

Cats are my most despised animals, and knowing these pets belonged to my hated enemy my prejudice for these furry critters grew even more. I realized if they could actually speak they would beg me to put them out of their misery but with the LSD still effect-ing my body, they literally did so.

I suggested my idea to my favorite followers, but they declined the theory explaining how cruel that would be, knowing I would fulfill my humble plans even if they didn't. Bradley sat undecided about my plan, but he knew there were no substitutes of what we could do, and Brad knew he wouldn't be the field man in this little prank, just an accomplice.

The Bronco halted in the center of a black asphalt trail then turned around traveling twice as fast as when we were fleeing. Seconds before rushing past Steven's sorry domain I ejected the black creature out through the front window, as it hit the leaning mailbox at a life-stealing thud. My pals and I reported with laughter, as the black furry victim jumped up for seconds, only to run aimlessly then fall in his chosen resting place. Bradley retreated down the road for a moment to insure our stealth concepts were still in action then turned around, as he handed me the next being to be put out of his misery. This time I merely threw the full-grown kitten at the rushing curb that was on the opposite side of the street, where his death-sharing victim laid. We all watched the hilarious situation as the living creature rolled across the hard surface, braking the speed with fur that scraped off skin. Both of the freak's pets laying across from each other in a thanksgiving of rest, in that I granted them peace from a despicable and shaming master.

The Bronco hurried off leaving this problem solving crime scene to authorities that would try their hardest in forcing the public to believe that they would do everything possible in apprehending the culprits.

I would have paid money for the look of Steven's crying face when his abusive parents made him fetch the morning paper that day. God would be happy to see the nerd crying over creatures that probably served a finer purpose in life than him, as he supposedly does the right thing by reporting it to the protecting and serving cops, that would arrive two hours later just to say, we're on it. Oh, how grand it would be to witness the shocked freak stain his hands from the blood of his loving pets as he carried them to a proper burial.

After the adrenaline rush left and when the talk of a different subject than cats began to emerge, my addiction for alcohol rose above anything else on my mind. The clock reminded me that all of my buyers were either sleeping or topping their long day's work in an envious tavern forcing myself an underage beer retrieving hypothesis. My tiny imagination prevented me from any real foolproof plan but without complaints of the present company, we together agreed on my simple idea.

The black automobile pulled into a customer deserted gasoline station and was parked on the side of a pre-paying pump to pose as the everyday normal customer. I entered this miniature grocery structure, while smiling at the unsuspecting older clerk that greeted my decision of his store, not realizing I picked this establishment knowing security cameras wouldn't be a problem. Seconds later, Travis entered, then questioned the teller in prices of the surrounding items he wouldn't purchase, doing a fine job in following the plan with his diversion.

I quickly located the beer section of the security lacked mini mart, then wiped my watering mouth, knowing how soon my body would again taste alcohol. I grabbed two cases of beer, while listening to my loyal spy trade thoughts with some working old man that was forced a graveyard shift. With both the alcoholic treasures in my hands, I turned around to a laughing clerk that probably trusted my pal Travis with his life, never underestimating the strong weapon of humor. With a friendly smile on my face, I slowly directed myself towards the front counter and when I was a couple of feet from my assumed destination, I made a quick dash for the exit. I threw open the swinging door then ran my fastest towards the getaway vehicle that sat two laughing people, who now screamed out phrases of encouragement. I sat myself in the black revving truck, then watching Travis arrive to seat himself in the back. In something that felt like hours we fulfilled my scary plan in less than a minute, receiving a prize that would totally compensate for all the trouble.

Wasting no time at all I gave myself a more than suitable stolen beer, but it wasn't really stolen—only to the mindless barbarians that established drinking laws, was it stolen. The government that voted drinking ages in, are terribly successful thieves in that this gullible old man would have received the correct payment for his beer if ages didn't matter. In this single area, the law robs two people, one of their money and one of the fantastic feelings of alcohol. I can tell you the corrupt side of law did not steal from the righteous today, drinking down the beer that tasted a million times pleasing, believing I was victorious in a small battle with the law.

Excusing of the Prince

I was not informed of the false accusations until Monday, since I spent the remaining weekend with my beloved prize, now growing to uncharted levels of affection towards her. Unlike the majority of my past girlfriends, I have truly started to develop strange and unexplainable feelings for her very existence. This relationship has endured longest of all other past flings, as I grow on presenting her with popularity, while she knows the highlights of life by giving in to both of our sexual desires.

First period did not even begin when I first heard of the falsified rumors, which had already infected the entire student population. The information that I acquired framed Bradley, as a horrible disliked criminal that will now unfortunately be classed near Steven, in the long ladder of popularity. It was bizarre witnessing the prince and second in command of school tossed so far away from the popularity that was once taken for granted. He was a respected man and did not deserve such treacherous lies bestowed on him. My sidekick did not deserve the outstanding fines, crooked law officials forced him to pay. He did not deserve to have his vehicle number witnessed by traitors of humanity or Steven's wicked neighborhood.

Rumors accused him for stealing alcohol then directing himself towards Steven's home while intoxicated, only to drive on the sidewalk, through a field, and on Steven's front yard. Rumors also explain the death of four or five cats killed due to drunk driving which wasn't that tragic even if it were real, but I was also foolishly told of smeared traces of blood that spelled out threatening vulgarities, located on the sidewalk. The world is a nasty place where humanity punishes those who help defenseless misguided animals and prevent the underaged folk of an entertaining day.

Bradley was no longer recognized as a human being in the perspective of classmates and females that now feared him. He was a nerd, freak, geek, loser, idiot, or reject. My definition of these phrases probably served the most use, since living as a disliked figure was the very opposite of my school career. They were anyone different, anyone strange enough to pose as annoying. Different was believing in morals, knowing morals do not exist in the current world. Different was anyone who prevented in achieving a life of a winner. Living the life of a winner meant the infatuations of the opposite sex and the simple ability to comfortably socialize with others. Winners were the best in everything and gained the admiration of others by being the people everyone wanted to be. We have great looks, strength, disrespect, and irresponsible traits, but we are the chosen holy children, so God looks out for us. The planet is a place for amusement and losers will try to disrupt that flow of entertainment with the puzzling routines that they call, the right way. A nerd is anyone who does not and attempts to resemble me.

During that Monday nobody spoke to Bradley or even gave him a simple hello. Facial expressions of hatred carried on that entire week and it was not for a month until my misunderstood friend tricked the opposite sex in communicating with him. As Bradley's popularity depleted the contact I shared with him was only fulfilled on the weekends. He was still my most favorite of companions, but he lost the popularity that allowed him to be seen with me. On a scale of being hip Bradley only made me look bad so conversing with him in front of the school's public became completely unacceptable.

It happens to everyone, people will one day find themselves in sitting observations of their once friend, pass their everyday familiar lunch table acting the role of not noticing their pal, who watches a best friend and new enemy walk past them to sit with the winners. I pity but shun my right arm even though he loyally prevented us from being branded as psychos and accepted all of our responsibilities of breaking the so-called law, for which I so humbly thanked him.

Brad's Chapter

How could he do this to me? I've known Mic my entire life and now he treats me like he doesn't even know who I am. He actually goes out of his way to not be caught with me or socialize with me where others might see us. How could Mic betray me like this? I trusted him with my life and I would have done anything for him. Now I don't think I can trust anyone ever again. I didn't even do anything wrong. He was the one who threw the cats out the window; I didn't even want him to. Now I'm blamed for everything, everyone in school hates me and I have a whole bunch of fines to pay. Now I am forced to sit here in school and eat lunch with the nerds. They're not that bad of people once you get to know and talk with them. I remember coming to school that first day I, as the most hated person in school. I went to find a place to eat, thinking I would be eating alone and despite what these guys heard about me, they asked me if I wanted to eat with them. These people really give you that sense of honesty. I mean it's like if you asked them to do something they would do it. They also give off that vibe of caring, not like any vibe Mic gave off.

There were three of them, and they were just arriving, since I always got out of my class earlier than most.

"What's up Brad?"

"Not much, Johnny."

John was a good guy, he was a bit whacked out in the head, but he was so loyal to his friends I was proud to have him sit next to me. He was carrying a brown lunch sack and he always sat to my right. He never did drugs, never got into fights, and he was always very shy.

"How you doing, Bradley?"

"Pretty good Pete, how about yourself?"

"I'm fine now that lunch has started."

Peter was always fun. He was the most perfect example of a nerd, glasses, zits, and a squeaky voice, but he accepted me no matter what he heard about me.

"What's up Bradley?"

"Hey, what's up Phil?"

Phil was a very morally good person. He actually cared for people for who they were. He was a real religious person and he was always doing things for his youth group.

Not one of my new friends ever had a girlfriend and I felt sorry for them. It wasn't their fault they were freaks, they were outcasts because life was so hard on them for so long it has scarred the way they think. They didn't know how to talk to people because most of the people that raised them were mean to them their whole lives. Now they live their warped lives trusting their friends as family members. I know I said I wasn't ever going to trust anyone again, but I do trust my new friends. Mic will always be my friend, but he can go to hell if he thinks he's better than anyone else.

BK's Chapter

I can't wait to tell my friends Mic's going to be mine, I hope. He's so sweet I want him so bad. I don't know what it is, but there is something about him that is just so charming. I can't wait to tell my friends. Once we get to my house I'll tell them, I'm going to have sex with Mic Wilson.

Katie drives so slow sometimes, thank God we're almost there. I've told her how to get to my house a hundred times and she still doesn't know the way.

"Take a right at the intersection, and after that just keep going until you reach the green bushes in front of my house."

The radio was playing Tammy's favorite song; she started dancing in the car so when in Rome, I started to dance too. Tammy was sitting in the back, while I sat in the passenger's seat. I could hear my friends singing along and before I knew it, we pulled up into my gray driveway, while Tammy and I still danced. The music played out loud and then we heard nothing, the car was turned off and it was time to return to my bedroom so I could tell my friends the great news.

We got out of the car and started for the front door. My house was brown with a tan trim, there were big round bushes in front of my yard and flowers surrounded my home.

I'm so glad that my parents both work, situations like these are so much more perfect.

I opened up the brown door and went in, my friends followed. I told them to make themselves comfortable, and get ready for the good news. I left for the bathroom, getting excited to tell my friends the great news. He was just so kind and a perfect gentlemen. He is the most thoughtful person in the world, that's probably why every girl wants him. After prom night he is going to want me and I'll have the most gorgeous guy in town, I hope. I wonder if he thinks I'm pretty, I wonder if he likes me, he probably doesn't even know who I am. I don't care, I have to have him.

I returned from the bathroom and told my friends to brace themselves.

"You know Mic Wilson don't you?"

"Are you serious? BK, he's like the most sweetest and hottest guy I've ever seen."

"Yea, and he's such a humanitarian too. He's so kind and gentle. There's not a girl in school that doesn't want him. Why'd you ask?"

"Well, I know this sounds a little crazy, but on prom night I'm totally going to have sex with him."

"What? And how are you going to do that?"

"I asked his friend Bradley to the prom. I'm pretty sure that they're all going to the dance together."

"You asked Bradley, he's such a jerk. He's so yucky, I could never do that no matter how bad I wanted someone."

"I sort of feel guilty for using Bradley, but then after what he did to Steven I'm guessing he might need to be taught a little lesson."

"What about his girlfriend, Jennifer?"

"What about his girlfriend?"

"You can't do that to her, she's such a sweetheart."

"Jennifer's a bitch, Tammy. She's totally dating him to be popular."

"Yeah, but they'll be all over each other all night long. You're never going to get the chance."

"I've thought about this already. Now Jennifer is just using Mic, and I'm sure he knows this. I'm thinking when Jennifer goes to the bathroom or something, I'll tell Mic how special he is to me, and then he'll want to be with me."

"How do you know he likes you, BK?"

"I don't, but we're perfect for each other, I mean isn't that enough? He's just so perfect."

"Bradley deserves to be taught a lesson, I mean everyone knows that, but I've talked to Jennifer and she really doesn't deserve what you're going to do to her."

"I know that Katie, but I think that there is one special person on this planet that was sent here just for you. There's one person that's perfect, and once you find that special someone, you shouldn't let him go. Jennifer isn't good for Mic, he should be with me. If I were a guy I would be him and if Mic were a girl he would be me. I almost feel like I love him, and I haven't even talked to him before. We were destined to be soul mates."

"So what if you tell him how you feel and he tells you he's in love with Jennifer."

"That can't happen and it won't happen. Mic wants me and I want him, I want him bad."

"Let me get this straight, you asked Bradley to the prom so you can have Mic. Sometime during the night you're going to ditch Bradley and confess your love to Mic, who is going to the prom with Jennifer. Then when you find Mic you're going to have sex with him, even though you've never talked to him before."

"To put it any simpler Tammy, I'm going to fuck his brains out."

Prom Night

Months passed by, as Jennifer and I continued as a couple, starting to really get serious, while I began to think of her when I awoke from sleep, then dream about her at night. I pursued in being the same Mick though; I was not that serious, since I would still be forced to say good-bye to her if she ever thought about not sucking my entertainment to her fullest potential. I simply say serious because I strangely desire Jennifer's company and the lasting relationship we share is staggering on a record-breaking time frame for me. I have suffered much, bringing Jennifer to all the school dances, playing my part as the perfect gentlemen, but that's only if she fulfilled her after-hour duties.

The ceremonial ritual of Senior Prom was held this Saturday and I was supposed to arrive with all of my humble associates, but arriving with Bradley was still questionable, knowing he still lacked a dance partner and also popularity. I planned to bring Kenny, Travis, Jason, their dates, and of course, Jennifer, who probably sat foolishly near her telephone, just waiting for the boyfriend signed call that would dissolve all her prom date worries. Jennifer serving as my prom date was a fact, I just enjoyed watching her sweat and nervously continue to open up the prom subject, as I would then reply, first I have to ask you.

My generous family gave me money for the original black tuxedo and a stretched white limousine that had all the Hollywood accessories, tinted windows, furry white upholstery, and a bottle of very expensive champagne. My band of companions would be retreating to my party afterwards, but the champagne just added to my romantic class and style.

Driving to this civilized hoe-down in one's car is so pathetic and I could not picture myself showing up in anything else, as I presently explain my theory of limousines already surviving through one prom night before.

My old prom date looked smashing in a dress and treated herself with a little more class than Jennifer, but the scenario of friends was totally reciprocated, as we both finished the cool night fortunately with our nude docking bodies, but unfortunately in absence of a party.

This night will be remembered for a lifetime and anybody who arrives in some daily driven vehicle that has the scent of school texts and some weird oil leakage problem should have enough reason to reject all thoughts of attending. Students in refusal of alcohol should not arrive to prom. Students that wait until marriage should not arrive to prom. Nerds should not attend and people who do not dance should definitely not go.

Jennifer put on her prestigious ballroom uniform and cleansed herself for the occasion, knowing my call would eventually conduct. I presented Jennifer with the prom date question only minutes before I brought my already prepared friends, including Bradley, and their swinging dates to her house. Jennifer was trying to act calm like she had another date, but anybody could see through her snobby disguise with the telephone answer of, it took you long enough.

Upon arrival caught a surprised glimpse staring out through a window, as Jennifer's blue eyes lit up in an impressive glare, watching her boyfriend arrive in a limousine she was not aware of. I exited out and knocked on my date's front door to retrieve her, when she threw open the entrance, looking so extremely lovely, focusing all her attention on the piece of wealth I painstakingly achieved to show off. She looked beautiful wearing a silvery light blue gown that made Cinderella look like a hillbilly and had her hair standing up just to add to the occasion. I slipped her the deserving corsage every girl took for granted then unfolded my next gift with a gentle kiss, followed by leading her by hand towards the long white automobile. She entered in first and sat right down next to Kenneth, leaving just enough room for me. I noticed my companions' dancing partners, rating them as I went along, thinking how lucky I was to have a girl that fit the look of a true prom date. Prom dates should fit the perfect description of the princess read about in fairy tales or else they should not attend this updated ball. Many will remember this date in time forever and it should not be ruined by the obese appearance of some lazy female that doesn't exercise. As I am admiring Jennifer's great looks and then turn my vision upon a round disgusting pig, my eyesight could literally be harmed to the point in leaving the dance early. This can happen to anyone and is just one of the reasons only the elite should be publicly seen at dances.

I looked across from me locating Bradley's familiar elegant catch staring right back, as I began to ponder my sweet thoughts for the semi-worthy date and question how Bradley, with his newer hated reputation, received a date with a body of such great stature. I recognized his prize as one of the host's of our school pep assemblies, she attended the school as long as I, but strangely never stopped to talk. Her name was once known but now forgotten, yet this tantalizing gown was widely known, but I lack the information of her name because of her stalling in communicating with me.

She continued to stare at me, as I turned to focus on my affectionate mate thinking and knowing how easy my next victory could be, but she was Bradley's belonging for the night, even though no one admired him.

Jennifer observed all the switches and compartments with the curiosity of a child, lifting up the telephone only to put it back down then climbing out the sunroof to say hello to all the passing people. I squeezed through the top of the automobile with my elegant piece, kissing her to the bright passing lights of a city, which supplied Jennifer with enough excessive happiness, that she finally found enough courage to thank me.

When arriving to our swinging destination everyone acted like the hot shots I usually portrayed myself to, as the limousine parked in front of a huge crowd of curious students questioning who was going to get out first. The chauffeur opened the exit allowing myself to receive the recognition I deserved and escape out into the stares of envious students that so much wanted my vanity. I humored the pathetic unfortunate souls with a waving of my hand, helping my glamorous-looking date out of my wealth then into a gigantic canopy of jealousy.

I said hello to more then a dozen friendly subjects, as I routed my short destination inside the front doors displaying my prom tickets to a past teacher that now posed as a bouncer. He was standing next to a door that hung colorful streamers when he nodded passing me the authorization to enter. Jennifer and I walked in an enormous world of fantasy watching hundreds of celebrating friends cling onto someone different all beneath the light of a glimmering disco ball. It was a darker structure but illuminated enough to witness who was all accounted for and there were decorative streamers that hung from walls then attaching to the ceiling.

We waited up for our tag along buddies, wondering what was making their arrival such postponement, so I told my waiting princess I would divert myself in search for them.

The huge crowd surrounding the entrance together strangely decided to enter in, developing a line that put my companions towards the end. So with all this extra time I had no choice but to locate a secluded area and drink the concealed present no one else knew about.

I went into the men's restroom and headed towards a vacant stall, while twisting off the cap of a small plastic soda bottle that was halfway filled with clear great tasting vodka. I quickly chose the white toilet housing near the end of the tiled room and began my night with the first consumption of alcohol that entire Saturday. The taste of this gift still burned my mouth and throat, but I forced the entire contents down, not knowing my next appointment with any type of liquid that supplied the effects of being intoxicated.

With a piece of sterilizing gum in my mouth I returned to the area of the dance floor discovering that
all my friends were present and already dancing. I
glanced towards Jennifer and asked her to join me in
the first slow dance of our Senior Prom, as she gave me
clearance by cradling my arm in explanation to lead
her out. I zigzagged through a few couples then
stopped in the area that all my buddies claimed and
stood slowly dancing. I developed into dancing position, then grinning at the facing ideal that smiled at
me and began to sway. With my hands around her tiny
waist she rested her head onto my shoulder, as I
sniffed in the pretty aroma of her perfume, turning
around to face Bradley's back and noticing his
so-called affectionate belongings again staring at my
understandably good looks. I watched her crack a
smile displaying her intimate feelings for me, as I
tossed her a simple wink of my eye then looked down
gently, touching Jennifer's soft hair with my cheek.

The song finished with the funky sounds of a
quicker beat transforming the floor into a humorous
dance contest that consisted of any school clown to
show off inside a huge ring of spectators. Everyone of
my friends were forced to partake in this sarcastic
show as they one by one jumped in the center of the
human ring, dancing in the most peculiar style possible. My fellow school mates met all the possible demands in the fittings of the dancing impaired and even
if they could show off in the steps of such a quick beat
all friends would decline, knowing that this ring was
merely a ritual of fun.

With my hand holding Jennifer's, she pulled me
near telling me to get out there and do something for
the crowd, so when the ring was empty I leaped in

swinging to the continuous chanting of my name. I kept moving to the ongoing shouts of "Mic Mic Mic," hearing people laugh and watched my prom followers shower me with encouragement. I located my laughing prize, approaching her in the departing of the ring as an explanation to others that my show was now over. As I left another dancer jumped in then another and another until the catchy song grew quieter then depleted, only to start off with a whole different set of slower tunes.

My short almost fulfilled intentions were grabbing Jennifer around her waist, automatically starting the next dance, but as our bodies touched Bradley intercepted me from behind and asked if he could have the splendid pleasure of dancing with the prettiest girl here. She smiled and humored him by presenting him with one dance, as I then met eyes with Brad's female companion, who definitely wanted nothing else but to dance with me. Being polite I asked her, even though I already knew the answer and we began to slowly sway, then communicate. The area that I asked about was filling me with much curiosity and would have been eventually explained that night, for I could not even conceive someone of her great looks caught with such a nerd. She flattered me with her cunning ways explaining a long devious plan that emerged with the knowledge of Bradley going to the dance with his best friend, the most gorgeous guy she has ever seen. I accepted her forward pickup line, telling this fine victory that if Brad declined the offer I would not, as the fabulous deprived child approached closer trying to press every part of her body up against mine. Her nickname was BK, she knew of the party afterwards and continued to ask me for a short rendevous outside behind this dancing structure, but realizing how easy I would be apprehended, I did not. The song ended with the beginning of another slow song, as I said goodbye to the delicious temptation, then making my way towards Jennifer and again, the next contestant of winning my affection confronted me.

This pretty face was a regular in wanting my infatuations, but she stayed untouched because of my busy schedule and also because of her shy characteristic trait that cast her as a poor winner of popularity. I tossed Jennifer a look of apology, then grabbed the unexpected contestant around the waist to begin twirling her to a huge impressive smile. We both talked, but my in-love dancer was unfortunately not as hospitable in expressing what she wanted as Bradley's date was, in that I realized pride prevented this poor female in blurting out wanting me without clothes and helpless so she could have her way. I knew my beloved beauty would definitely stumble onto my sexual innocent side issues if I were to score with those who haven't had their turn with me at the same party, but her invitation was granted with the mercy I kept for her desires.

When the song ended I was basically handed off to another anxious and jealous mind, as the process started all over again with me receiving another's sexual assumptions, then inviting that worthy piece to my drinking festivities. As time and I were passed on, the sexual motives of others were beginning to tempt my body to the boundary of thinking about nothing except for what Jennifer would later give me. I desired to locate her in explanation of my feelings so we could hurry and escape to the easing of my sexual urges.

I didn't reach my frustrated Cinderella until the

head chaperon interrupted the current-time ball to crown the Prom King and Queen, then allowing them the whole dance floor to themselves. Prom King was a no contest, given to me without any doubt from the entire school, but Prom Queen was a question between many.

I was called to the center of the floor in acceptance of my crown, watching the faces of girls trying to fight off all their nervousness. My desires for Prom Queen were truly directed for Jennifer, but my wishes and her feelings crumbled when the name BK was shouted out.

BK screamed as well as all her surrounding friends that stayed aloft, while she rocketed up to take her side as Queen. As her crowning took place my eyes met Jennifer's and I could see the horrible look of disappointment cast its shadow upon her. I watched her friends begin to comfort Jennifer as they watched BK and I join together as Prom King and Queen.

I knew that my losing territory would despise the next act I was about to fulfill, but with the crowd watching and all of their minds set in stereotyping me as a Godlike figure that would amaze them, I had no choice.

I recognized the song as it started out slow, but would eventually speed up until it was the perfect sound for showing off in advertising myself in a huge spectacle. We were being polite in a slow sway but as the beat began to unfold I spun her around then catching her hand as she resumed her stance. The crowd started to praise me when I eased BK off the floor swinging her in a circle around my body like we had rehearsed this tricky routine once before as two professional dancers. I flung her high rolling her in the air then gracefully catching my partner before the attack of the ground as the impressed Queen rested in my arms pursuing a perfect time to kiss a girl under different circumstances. People applauded my fantastic grand finale, as I helped the undeserving queen to her feet, who plastered me with a thrilling look of astonishment. Immediately after sending BK a simple, nice dance, I approached a more jealous and upset version of Jennifer, as the floor was once again flooded with the normal prom attendance.

I was dancing in torture a bit, trying every angle in making my date feel better, while my sexual temptations again troubled me and with even more suffering I watched disgusting females who could pass as cows. I let out a silent prayer to God for a miracle of elimination that would accidentally send these overweight wallflowers to slip on ground, hard enough in forcing them home. I constantly asked myself, why don't they just go home? As Prom ended, I focused all of my skills in cheering up this hated side of Jennifer, dancing with no one but her, the remainder of the night.

When this dancing shindig ritual ended, all of my arriving friends filled into the same seating arrangements as before, except Jennifer lacked the perky childlike behavior, which to her information was because she was tired. We all knew her horrible frustration sprouted from the strange crowning, which was somehow placed on the head of BK, a pretty-faced comedian who steadily stared in my direction, making me uncomfortable. I knew exactly what BK wanted, but I also realized that this would be the very issue to cure my sweet Jennifer of all her troubles in the dark clutches of losing the Prom Queen title.

The limousine was the leader of a long line of party

animal driven vehicles that contained all of my loyal drinking subjects My interior group laughed at all the remembered prom highlights, popping off the cork of the spraying champagne bottle, then pointing the opening towards a window in prevention of raining on others. I slid open a side compartment that housed a number of long-stemmed crystal glasses while reaching in then displaying a glass for everyone. I poured the liquid accommodating a sufficient amount for my undeserving pals as I watched the expensive mouth-watering drink bubble and splash on the bottom of everyone's crystal cup. Presenting myself with a larger dosage, I elevated my liquid dessert aloft, and decided to pose a toast for my depressed Jennifer. "To my sweet Jennifer, may her motivations for drugs and alcohol never stop." With a bit of laughter we chimed our drinks together then consumed down the delicious taste of wealthy alcohol. I offered those for a second round, but gladly few accepted, leaving more for me. As I tipped back the crystal container of this liquid treasure, I stared right down the neck of the glass noticing BK fixed on my every movement. She lifted her glass in my direction asking for another serving as I so humbly granted her one, finally discovering a single individual amongst the small crowd who demonstrated the respect of a premium drink that is rarely offered.

Before completely pulling up on my driveway I exited the wealthy vehicle to direct traffic towards the side accessway that led to my backyard. Once the parking issue stopped serving a problem I opened up my enormous party hangout and began the celebration that would be remembered forever. People started to enter, filling themselves from the twin beer kegs I just tapped, and I sipped small samples of brandy from a bottle that just stood with a family of dozen.

With my castle packed with hundreds of party folk and the more than worthy prom dates that tried their hardest in sending me the dancing assumption that they were the rightful deprivement that were supposed to be grabbing me in the intoxicated phenomenon of drunk dancing. I merely turned away, grasping Jennifer's hand then leading her away from the socializing group she stood with, and upstairs to the familiar room of pleasure. I took about five steps when my clumsiness and alcohol played a trick on me, forcing the sixth step away, resulting in an embarrassing fall. It would normally hurt, but I was so drunk I didn't even realize the laughter that sprouted from Jennifer when she helped me up.

As I led her up, my girl suddenly became horribly delusional, explaining a postponement in the sexual deeds that were properly succeeded every weekend. I knew it was the perfect time, with me far from sober and all of my fellow appreciators of alcohol, staggering to wall-thumping music. It was then I realized my beautiful Jennifer invaded my intellect with a brilliant challenge, which set my nude goals available only with the strategy, as if I've never seen her. She said she wanted her time to talk with her friends but what she truly wanted and challenged me to was a pick up line, romance, or a love story, so fictionally I too told her I just wanted to talk. What I really was planning to confront was the great subject that was delayed, but couldn't ponder why, since my stunning princess obviously wanted it bad with all her stress jabbing at her.

We both entered the closed room, then sitting on the foot of the bed, as I looked at Jennifer with watery drunken vision, that was making her even more pleasing to me than before. While we sat on the bed and before the first word was spoken I began the first step of intimacy by kissing her neck. With a strange unexplainable reaction she told me to stop and it was then I realized that this, so-called annoyed movement, was part of her hard-to-get challenge. I knew she was just asking for it so I mounted on top of her, while kissing every location of exposed skin. For some weird reason Jennifer kept reminding me of my drunkenness, playing her good girl role a little too far, pushing me off then complaining. I began to imagine absurd doubts that my gorgeous date was actually serious when she screamed out, "get off," but knowing who I was she couldn't have been. I was a winner, the Prom King, a football all-star, a female on the planet that dismissed the opportunity of succeeding with me in bed, lacked existence. So with all this known information I began reaching up through the bottom of Jennifer's dress, in plans to retire from the complication of silk panties, while she grabbed at my hands. I ripped down my own underclothes, as I plunged myself inside of her, waiting for Jennifer to finally realize, any second now, who she was so honorably getting naked with. Jennifer was now screaming out in what I thought at the time was a premature orgasm, as she began to dig her nails into my back, handling the feeling in her usual style.

In the middle of all this fun and constant screaming, the bedroom door flew open leaving my companion Bradley planted in the center of the doorframe. I rolled over as we both stared at the silent motionless figure of Bradley, who currently stared back.

Breaking the dead silence my pretty belonging stood up and approached Bradley in a strange confusion of crying. Her jittery hands cupped her bawling face, as she walked up to my interrupting friend who gently threw his arms around my date, then reminding me of my intoxicated role. They both left my drunken vision and I never spoke to Jennifer again.

Deep down I knew Jennifer might not have desired my sexual activities during the present moment but she always dealt with the magnificent feeling in the same manner, screaming and clawing at my back. I figure once I slipped up inside her a couple of times she would realize the orgasm she had been stalling on and give in to her temptations. I refused to allow Jennifer to expose my anger although what truly enhanced my temper was a desperate resistance of the pleasurable feeling I was granted whenever I desired. Most females would not have to think twice about losing their virginity to me.

So with my traitorous Delilah strangely departing along with my nerdy friend, I watched a head pop into the empty space where the door usually stands when closed, and at that instant I recognized BK only horribly intoxicated, still wearing her glistening crown. She blurted out a slurred hello, stumbling towards me, depending on the walls and dressers to prevent herself from falling on her face. With the alcohol in her system BK was unaware of the previous abnormal episode with Jennifer, who slightly filled me with sadness coming from a bizarre unknown source.

She could hardly speak, but tried her best to express her feelings towards me in a completely not understood mumble, which was totally compensated for when her lips connected with mine. Being the Prom King I had no choice but to allow the Queen her right in fulfilling the sexual activities she had desired for so long.

After reaching climax we both escaped from each other, knowing that Bradley may show up later in the evening. So I stayed lying on my great sleeping battleground as BK retreated to locate her needs. While looking up at the white ceiling I was greeted by a forgotten party animal that had previously shared a dance with me that night. She was also drunk and entered in the similar style as BK, staggering and holding onto furniture. The process of kissing and ripping each other's clothing off repeated again and later with another contestant, as I just laid back thinking, Jennifer who? Oh, I was the Prom King.

Fair Time

Like every other regular population a yearly fair would concernedly return to my necessities, in that the rides, games, food, and fresh selections of country girls would refrain myself from a nervous breakdown.

Oh, how I love the annual state fair and its band of following carnies that opened up an adult recess for all those with a life of hardship, such as myself. My life patterns sometimes lead astray the desires of being civilized, but fortunately this pavilion of entertainment provided a local vacation away from all my responsibilities in parties and accessing alcohol for the thirsty.

My loyal favorites and I refrained from school the entire week the Amusement Park visited, mostly to ensure that my arising stressful madness would be subdued.

Since, I would never permit myself to squander my hard working money on such foolish things my friendly team began every fair day by cheating the entrance and ride stamps, with Jason's ability of sketching with felt markers. I sent my humorous associate, Travis out to memorize the stamp presentation by communicating with those who have already agreed with the six-dollar policy. Everyday the stamp would change in color and object so the knowledge of what Travis observed was highly important. Jason usually accompanied him to get a better idea, then draw the picture onto our hands.

Each day my companions and I would con our entrance to experience the view of a twirling world from dizzy rides. We all would spend hours on rides, never feeling the nauseous sickness that most people do. When the rides reached a dullness for that day my buddies usually made the effort of winning or stealing prizes from gambling booths. They were mostly run by talented folk who knew nothing about the world except for the strange ability of knocking down milk jars and throwing baseballs in metal jugs, making it look so easy. I would mingle with the wrangler-wearing farm girls that showed up to express how healthy their fat pet cow was. Weekdays at the fair mostly consisted of rides and food tasting, but the fun truly started near the end of the week, since the majority of my fellow classmates were weak and decided to not attend the festivities until they established assurance that playtime would not lessen their silly grades.

This particular Saturday night my comrades and I felt a bit of mischief collecting up within our minds, as a full moon floated overhead calling out our slowly surfacing freedom. I also felt a clan of violent behavior brewing about that usually sprung from publicly notifying one's incapacities, masterminded by my comedian Travis.

That was the reason Travis was allowed to follow me, his mere face meant laughter to many and even his most compact state of atoms were insults directed into the mental wounds or others, lasting forever on one's soul. Any statement expressed by Travis always gave others the notion to brand my companion as nothing but crazy. His insults could drive one mad enough to act out in foolish violence, humorous to watch and always more fun to react to, since not one of my friends would suffer a beating from anyone else except for me. He was a funny guy, but I continued to ponder his mad gestures, questioning if he was truly acting or not.

As my disciples prowled along the happy fair grounds, giving salutations to all of my horny puppets, I began to indulge myself in all of the screams and laughter from the surrounding rides, locking my mind in a humorous daydream that propelled a swinging Ferris wheel off its circular motion and rolling on top of retreating people. It would be a sight to capture the wheel rolling down the highway passing up cars, as news helicopters followed and yelled out, "what a disaster folks." The observant freezing in horror, as parents would shout at their children to quiet the atmosphere of nonsense involving a runaway Ferris wheel.

I shook my thoughts out of its hilarious skit and simply focused on the wheel's spectacular outline of fluorescent lighting, trying not to capture the offending view of couples announcing their love to the world, by grasping each other's hand in what they pathetically no doubt believe is amusing. They have grown up observing lovers on television, happy in the presence of their significant other, so by logic girlfriend and boyfriend will discover happiness when holding each other's hand. It was a foolish physical statement for most, but watching these silly love partners stare and humor each other, I smiled to the brilliant calculations of my next satisfactory idea.

First I stated my options, weeding out the improbable couples for my next bragging deed. The perfect scenario would be two arguing couples that were followed by a number of guy friends, but how could one find a thing in such a get-along atmosphere.

After a moment of my couple audition, I narrowed the decision down to the pair that would evidently react to the largest commotion. The choice was granted to a group of youthful rap wannabes, they acted tough as if they had just walked away from the very heart of the ghetto.

The decision couldn't have been given to a better group of people then the ignorant inspiration of nineties trial gangsters, as they walked along communicating to each other, expressing the usage off f-u-c-k between every other word. I hated these people, as they convinced most they hate growing up in the hood even though they never have, still they desire a bibliography of the streets enough to revolve their life into acting it. They were impostors, admiring the lifestyle of pimps, drug dealers, and a lady's man, if only they turned to me and would have discovered the true thing.

There were eight of them looking the exact same in their dark clothing, strutting by, avoiding any movements that made others comfortable. Instead the tough wannabe's labeled their public exposure as dangerous and violent, scaring away the innocent. The only female in the group had her attractive highlights, with her long waistline blonde hair and baggy clothing. Her head was covered with a gray stocking cap that was pulled down over eyes caked with mascara. In her left hand she carried a bag full of pink cotton candy and her right hand was protected by a bigger and more male version of her. He was cloned to her style of outer wear, all except for the makeup, hair and black baseball cap that he wore facing sideways. He was the fearless general in his group of savage idiots, leading his army nowhere with clenched fists, oh so disturbing my peaceful attitude with wants of breaking his face.

I hurriedly volunteered Jason in being the point man towards my next act of mischief, as he of course, excitedly accepted. With my buddies, I would occupy an audience-like view when Jason would approach the group of tough guys in accomplishing our amusement, trying his best to stop from laughing.

We all waited for my swift star, laughing at the estimated effect he would cause. We also tried not to be obvious in watching the selected group, as we finally located Jason quickly marching towards the point of our focused intention, fashioning himself to the manner that serviced the look of accomplishing a task of emergency.

He cut through the tiny crowd of Mafia youth and proceeded directly to the love struck fools with an incomplete setting on his face, then inappropriately broke the cuddly sick occasion by depositing a quick deep kiss on the female player of the useless relationship game. As Jason began sprinting away, the woman player stayed positioned and responded in laughter, but the male player reciprocated her feelings in mad anger protesting out, as he ignored the past prevention of displaying his animal rage to his favorite female, and followed his girlfriend's violator in a violent spree.

I nearly crouched over in painful laughter, watching the small form of sexual abuse answer back to the retreat of my laughing jackal, as he ran away from about eight different revengeful beings. Of course, I resumed with my role and led my team towards the commotion in protection of any harm that fell upon my valued Jason. We were in pursuit of the pathetic rioting culprits when they all escaped behind a semi-truck, and out of the public's sight. The little gang probably thinking that this form of concealed beatings are the first steps in an organized crime conspiracy that would eventually lead each of them in being some type of Mafia leader.

I circled my friends around the gigantic truck and into the view of twisted bullies who began torturing one of my most loyal associates with a fisting to his face. It was done, the assault was made, driving my humble kind state of mind into a rabid non-thinking pulse of eradication. My head throbbed with furious anger, making it impossible for me to recognize the extent of my outgoing injuries upon others, or who I was destroying. This single act of stupidity registered as an appointment of departing respect, as my side wasted no time talking or compromising and attacked the bad guys.

Just before my fist connected with the face of the closest available opponent, one of the wannabes announced my presence in a loud recognized, Mic Wilson. A distinguished crack arose, as my falling punching bag grabbed his bleeding nose in a moan that translated the fighter down and out. My friends chose their victims, as I turned to the closest non-fighting and fortunately their leader, giving him the silent assumption of being next on the list of punishment. My opposing warrior began begging me to cease, when I nailed him above the right eye, and continued to swing my knuckled weapons at his body. I watched my rival turn his back to me when I struck his right kidney, hearing him shriek in pain, then cowardly run off. I turned to focus on my next enemy, glancing to the portrait of my team's already surfacing victory, all except for Bradley who was currently dealing with outnumbered factor.

He was on all fours, as two attackers kicked his face and stomach area, taking advantage of the situation to their convenience. I hated to see my once favorite reduced in such ways, but it ended now, as I threw a sucker punch at the unobserving cheater, knocking him to the ground with a loud crack of his jaw. I kicked the other enemy, but it was blocked, as I tried again and again, allowing Bradley enough time to recuperate up. I observed my opponent's movements to decide my next attack when Bradley entered the fight by hitting his torturer in the stomach, knocking the wind out of his body.

Out of nowhere, I felt a sharp pain near my foot, immediately positioning around to view the return of my fighting coward, only this time he held a stick resembling a broom handle, in his hand. His offensive action hurt tremendously, but only damaged myself in making me madder, as I dodged his next blow to my head. He swung again, but I ducked downward, reporting back with an uppercut to his jaw that knocked him backwards and to the ground.

I jumped towards him and hammered both my feet in his face, probably knocking him unconscious, but I couldn't truly tell, so I continued to kick his bloody face until he was unrecognizable. I observed his every pore ooze out blood with every connection of my thrusting foot, then viewing his sideways misplaced nose spew out some type of white body fluid, thankfully pleasing my rage to a slow. Beating my opponent's face was productive, but became redundant with the girlfriend showing up, then mercifully screaming for her boyfriend's mutilated appearance. I halted and glanced at her, then switching to the sight of my associates battering down mushy flesh, not totally convinced we were victorious.

I was done fighting for one day, but when I glanced back for a second I saw that in the loyal girlfriend's horror the female had dropped the present of cotton candy her ugly boyfriends had purchased. I realized that this female homey was serving a state of shock that declined her of eating, so with the fear of expiring food I took advantage of my lust for the candy only received once a year, and saved it from being wasted. I realized my pale and scared spectator would not retaliate in anyway so I gave her no concern of threat, claiming the bag of sweets, and began consuming.

As I cherished in my sweet victory feast, I made the effort to round up the good guys who kicked their downed motionless fighters to a bloody mess. There were a few with broken bones, a few with deep cuts, but I merely grinned to witness the wrong crowd of tough guys adjust and accept their disrespectful defeat as crying sissies.

I called for my friends to abort these unintentional self-defense war fields, watching them wipe the blood off their knuckles and proving who was truly tough by leaving this silly crime scene unharmed.

As we started our escape, which meant any location except for the fair grounds, I began going over the violent episode that was just experienced, thinking why. It was not as if I had shared any feelings for my losing enemies, but this whole violent scene could have been prevented if they had just acted like civilized humans and talked it out. Would it have been too difficult to lay aside our revengeful instinct, and deal with anger in a compromise? I once heard the saying, eye for an eye, I am sure Jason would not have been offended by a gentle kiss from the lucky trash that had first received a kiss from him. Instead the temptation of violence was given into, and as a small gang now produced thoughts of changing their ways, each one of them telling themselves, maybe I should of just passed up on my tough guy routine. Still, it was always more fun this way.

As I led a real gang to the exit of this carnival, we came across my old pal Officer Stanley, who was probably watching for evil doers that may be the arousing trouble, like people who enjoy starting fights. I haven't seen my clueless friend in ages, so I thought it would be nice to catch up on all the good times.

I've known Officer Stanley, since my freshman year in high school when I gratefully saved thousands of students by pulling the fire alarm. No one knew of my accidental school fire, but with a bit of quick thinking no one was hurt, and Stanley awarded me for my heroic acts of bravery.

I confronted my old friend with a handshake, then asked him how the life of a police officer was. He greeted me back and mentioned how much his favorite quarterback had grown, then started the same ongoing conversation of criminals I should not get myself involved with. He talked of drugs, alcohol, violence and how I should revolve my life around them, truly convincing himself these joyful issues were horribly unmoral, but what my kind law protector failed to know was that most of his conversation pieces wouldn't even exist if it weren't for me. I always thought it was ironic to befriend myself with a figure of such opposite of life's basics that tried to keep myself away from people like me. He slowly spoke about the subject of violent teenagers being rushed to the hospitals and he was merely searching the leaving kids for any blood marks or evidence of assault.

I was more than pleased to find that the defeated tough guys realized who was at fault and didn't apply my name, probably because they knew their home would be burnt to the ground when they returned from their medical recuperating destination. I told the friendly officer of my theory on how we should all act as civilized humans and compromise our anger, then ending my words with, "I hope you catch the evil monsters you're looking for."

Sheriff's Chapter

Why can't all kids be like that? Now that is a kid I am proud to have in my town. Not like the trouble-making punks, kind of like the kids that were sent to the hospital. If only I knew who did that, I don't know if I would arrest them or shake their hand.

I can't wait to see that Mic off to some University. The kid's going to make me proud and give us something to talk about when he's at it. Thank God the fair's over now all I have to do is get to my car, drop Jake off and go home.

"Deputy Jake, you know that Mic Wilson don't you?"

"Yes sir I do."

"Well remember that kid because he's going make us all proud. He's a great kid, hell of a throwing arm too. Wish all teenagers could be like him. Oh, the car's over here rookie."

"Throwing arm, sir?"

"Yea, the kid can go to any college he wants. He'll be playing for the professionals some day. And you know why deputy?"

"I'm afraid I don't, sir."

"The kid never cheats, never steals, never been to a party and got drunk. The boy never touches drugs and the kid never lies. He's everything I want in a son. Yep, his father should be damn proud."

"That sounds great, sir. Do you want me to drive?"
"No, I can handle it."
"The boy sounds perfect, sir."
"Well he is."

Graduation

My daily high schooling torture finally came to an end, as I slipped on my red graduation cap and gown, knowing this was the beginning day of the rest of my life, to party hard. I was more than grateful to get out of school and into the so-called real world. I would celebrate this new responsible world all summer and return back to school in the fall, but this wasn't ordinary school. I would be attending a University to partake in everything I enjoyed in high school only twice as much, and also play football on the side.

The awakening of this final day brought alcohol and girls from morning twilight, miles from the city on some student's secluded piece of farm property. Though this alcoholic celebration did not sprout from my touches, it was still party-worthy with its fascinating attendance number and wide selection of liquor products. Beer was already expressing its works throughout my body, as I thumbed through a Steven-engraved yearbook that Jason previously handed me. The acquiring of my rival's yearbook was left a mystery but what my humble disciples and I were about to do was clear and completely logical.

All I needed was a permanent writing utensil to sketch obscene vulgarities all over Steven's yearbook, so he will remember his disgraceful life when he moves into his new one. My friends drew simple phrases of hate, which was more than entertaining, but I felt I had to be a little more creative in my fun.

I was nominated to speak along with our class's valedictorian Steven, so I thought the best way to criticize my less than worthy arch nemesis was to print my good-bye speech on the front page of his annual. When it was time for me to speak I would walk up with his yearbook, place it on the podium, then leave it there for Mr. Steven.

When it was time to arrive at the destination of accepting my diploma, I was far from sober enough to drive but I could walk semi-straight and speak a little. My speech was currently slurring after the trial of every sentence, but one could still understand it some. I could walk without falling, but everyone automatically realized I had been drinking, which was probably ok in the eyes of most authority figures, being graduation day and all. Before I left I filled my disposable drinking cup to the top and carried it with me, sipping the great taste every chance I had.

Wearing our graduation uniforms we all piled into Kenny's pickup as he drove along the dusty country trail that eventually led to the highway, which directed the vehicle back to the school. The ceremony took place behind the school on the nice clean football field. There was hundreds of white folding chairs lined up parallel to each other and a podium which displayed a microphone that was hooked up to a sound system, surrounding all of us. We had rehearsed the graduating routine previously in the day but it accomplished close to nothing. I was aware of when I was to speak and when I was to accept my diploma, so I did not have to rehearse nothing else. All I found myself to care about was the delicious satisfying liquid that I now sipped between any bumps in the upcoming driving roads.

We drove up into the school parking lot as Gods, with the stereo system blasting so loudly it marked our arrival. We were piled in, standing up, then screaming out wildly, partly because of our graduation and also because we had returned. My attendance had to be known.

I involved myself in communication with a few, then took my white lawn chair as once rehearsed. I sat between two strange gentlemen that escaped from the same party as I. I could smell alcohol on both of them, which was in no question the same aroma that sprang from me. The chairs were set up so we faced the crowd, which consisted of happy parents who would also be drinking tonight in celebration of ridding themselves of their loved but frustrating children.

Children were also an odd annoying aspect that would never happen to me. It was pathetic to see parents raise something as their first priority when the child moans about his life and hates his parents. The kid would either grow to respect his parents in wanting their support or grow to reject the respected support of his parents. There is never an in-between, this is why I have chosen to allow myself entertainment and the welcoming of a non-children life. My parents raised me properly giving me freedom and complete trust in my growing life.

I noticed the crowd in locating my parents, as they watched their drunken heir listen for his cue to address the audience and departing high school students, in an educational good-bye. It sometimes angered me to watch some parents look at their pathetic children in hopes of their only chance of delivering themselves out of poverty and suffering. Some students destroy their entire future with silly ideas of computers and other directions of nonsense, crushing any plans of making a family proud to have an adult child.

The ceremony began with the standing of our nation's theme song, then followed by a few words from our deceiving principal, as the never again respected authority figure announced fictional phrases of sorrow in observing his pupils abandon the school to better things. The principal left the podium with a small amount of applause from only the parents, but echoes of roar disrupted my eardrums, when I took the stage in comforting my fellow school. I stood in front of the podium, noticing my surprised guardians admire the unknown popularity of their only child, as I reached out my hand across the crowd in a sideways motion, to quiet them down. I could not blame them though, they recognized me as more dominant giving me the amount of exalt they desired and also the amount I deserved. It was now quiet and everyone listening realized my intoxicated state, but failed to care, telling themselves it was fine to drink on graduation day.

"I remember trying to get a drink out of the school's drinking fountains and strain on the tip of my toes to take a sip. Now it's like I have to bend all the way over for my hips to reach the water. I've been told when I was young I would have to eventually grow up then live amongst the grown-ups and I said fine. So as I was getting out of bed this morning I told myself, this was the day . . . Good-bye and remember me."

My worshiping audience laughed even more as my hired pizza deliveryman walked through the vision of everyone's eyesight and handed me a pizza then said,

"$10.99." It took a fifty-dollar tip to convince this fool into doing this embarrassing interruption, but fifty dollars was a minute sacrifice for the amount of laughter that now praised me.

After I was given the pizza I sent out a simple sophisticated good-bye, then left the podium, and also Steven's annual. As I left, every single person exploded with applause for me, but a shrieking silence followed when Steve's turn to speak began. Steven ran up in front of an audience of hatred, surprised by the annual that left him standing with a speechless lame expression on his ugly face. He started to flip through the pages to observe his already known hatred, as the waiting graduating parents began to get frustrated. I began with laughter when he shortened his speech to a smaller extent of mine, then hurried off the stage to his chair, in a frightened escape. I realized he had stage fright but I know Steven left because he didn't want to cry in front of his fellow classmates because somebody drew graffiti all over his frozen memories in time. Like all my other school buddies I was glad, we all had a huge party waiting for this long pointless ceremony to end.

It was a long treacherous wait but with the help of the working alcohol I was able to sit without going totally mad. It came to the point where we threw up our hats then went outside to say so long and take photographs. I was conversing with one who was qualified for my flirtation when my most disgusted enemy confronted me with tears and asked me, why. He then explained his strange plans of loving his enemies then asked if he could pray with me.

I could not believe that this nasty parasite believed his prayers would even be considered good enough for me. I looked him in the eyes and felt the anger I would so love to act upon him with. Oh, how I felt like striking him down as he stood before me, but under the current circumstances, with a number of people staring I settled with a quiet phrase of threat that no one else heard, then followed by accusing him of being less than any creature that existed.

He left as I continued my flirting, when my father confronted me, and shook my hand, passing me a white envelope. My father said I earned it, surprising me with a four-day cruise to some Jamaican paradise that would leave the next morning. Like anyone else, I was ecstatic with happiness, giving both of my guardians a gigantic hug and a simple pose for their picture. With my cruise in one hand and my other hand reaching around the tiny waist of an attractive goal, I departed this time-wasting ritual and returned to the more suitable party.

The Real World

I can say with ease that my normal years in high school were not as similar to the surrounding population. I was a reigning star, and my educational life was so incredibly easy, but at the time I was happy it was. After my cruise I attended college due to my arts of football. College was, by far, a different scenario than high school. The amount of women, parties, and alcohol delivered themselves daily, and in much higher numbers. I couldn't have been more pleased, as everything was drawing itself fine, until I lost my scholarships during my second year because of an ignorant decision from a higher official, who insanely decided that drunkenness was not the answer. I was then dismissed from that college, and was not able to regain another scholarship, forcing me to work. It did not bother me though, as long as parties and women were in my life I could care less about any hardships. Some say I was very fortunate when I received a high position from my father, but I hated it. A lot of the people I knew in high school still helped my depressing work life, by partying, and during these days I finally achieved the long awaited age of twenty-one. I again began to enjoy what I had with all of my girlfriends and alcoholic celebrations. Life was great until my very own father fired me because of his filthy beliefs in keeping a company together. If there was anyone on this planet that wouldn't betray me and also understand my method of passing the day away, I would have guessed it to be my father, but I was wrong. My father explained the reason for my sudden layoff was due to his terms of bad work habits, in which he hated a few minutes late, and returning to work with a few beers in one's system. Another one of his so-called bad work habits did not happen perpetually, but he hated his phone lines filled with calls of my future pleasures.

No one had the authority to act upon me in this manner, not even my father. I did not strike at him, but with a bit of rage I deservedly shouted at my father, until I was not forgiven, and forced to move out of my comfortable already paid for life, which provided food, clothes, and an automobile.

I stayed in a wide selection of homes belonging to my friends and past victories, who still wanted me. I would settle at the home of a prize piece when the female that so wanted me began to transform weak and pathetic, telling me she hated the lifestyle I led and also explained that she had no idea I was one who lived in the style that she hated. My current pleasurable landlord would start to reject my intimate compliments, grow angry, and call me some type of disgusting fool with no plans to better myself, but most females were lost. I discovered there was a surprisingly huge amount of losers that were never accounted for as I was kicked out of one home and into the next. Every girl failed to ease my temptations making her expendable, and most of my pretty housemates would turn lazy to even reject a small task as driving me to a desired destination. This went on for months, as I tried to acquire employment at different locations, one location most memorable out of all of the rest.

I traveled by bus to a local gas station in response to an interview, which was a complete waste of time, for I was overqualified for the position. As I entered the miniature food depot I was confronted by, none other then the gullible chump I once burglarized.

It turns out that this gullible working freak owned a gigantic branch of gas stations, and I just happen to direct myself in wanting employment from him.

He recognized me in the same degree, as he asked if I enjoyed the stolen beer, then threw me outside, after hitting me in the stomach and face.

I allowed him the few cheap shots, mostly because I feared the threat of being apprehended by the police, and evacuated the hostile scene immediately. Still, I enjoyed life with my still lasting popularity as my old loyal companion Bradley took pity on his best friend, and gave him the opportunity of staying at his small trailer for absolutely free. I forgave him for defending Jennifer and he delivered his apologies by laying out a free area to rest for awhile.

It was strange watching old classmates pursue hard straining lives and pick career choices that settle them into a life of constantly reoccurring daily happenings, following them until they die. My own favorite disciple Bradley had gotten himself married, forcing him to work in support of his forever responsibilities. I once told Brad to never lie down and rest in the ritual that would last a lifetime, but some cease to ever listen and learn. I became a bit frustrated not being able to witness their marriage, I was happy for Brad, but then a part of me couldn't care.

I slept on a cheap brown couch, as Brad and his

wife fell asleep together, as newlyweds. He supported his new significant other by working in a factory a few miles out of town. His lovely wife stayed home, and took care of the cozy place. I was unemployed for months, as I continued to search for other than working in fast food and minimum wage.

One day while sitting on my brown bed, probably annoying Brad's wife, an ad in the newspaper caught my attention. It called for a hard-working person that could slave away in a high school for twelve-fifty an hour. I called and set up an appointment, which took place on the seventh floor of a very successful computer company. My desperate need for money was so great I failed to care for the knowledge of what I would be straining myself with, but a hard worker is all the ad was calling for.

About two days later I groomed myself presentable for the interview, then begged Bradley's soul mate for a ride over to the opportunity that veiled its twelve-fifty an hour duty.

Arriving at the spectacular building, that opened its mouth to an infinite stampede of workers, walking, as zombies toward the entrance, I sliced through the crowd, and asked for directions at the service counter.

I located the elevator, and borrowed its quick upward transportation to a clean room with chairs, one gigantic window, and a very attractive secretary. I watched the beautiful office manager stand up then greet me with a huge smile and a black mini skirt, housing two perfect legs.

She threw out her hand, introducing herself by, "You must be Mic."

I said yes, then was told to take a seat, as I sucked

in tasty perfume aromas, ever so wanting to suck down more than just smells.

Waiting for the leading employer that would see me shortly, I watched all that was governed by the neighboring mystery man, through the window of this towering magnificent structure. Oh, how great it would be when I would have finally reached the point in life to execute authority over all, in a place similar to this.

I realize the person inside the adjacent office did actually own all leadership of every item that was planted in the great view I focused on. He probably once resembled me with his superb choices in secretaries and outstanding location of offices. With a fine-looking skirt like that you would have to be strong, intelligent, and very good-looking.

The gorgeous secretary interrupted my daydream, telling me that I may now have the pleasure in meeting the great man who has rule over every movement in this computer typing labor camp. Finally being able to observe what was on the other side of the office door, I walked in. I could have died. There he was, sitting in a leather-revolving chair, looking up at me with a confident smirk. He looked extremely different, but still resembled his teenage facial traits enough to be recognized. He was wearing a nice suit and his hair was all slicked back resembling some kind of movie star. His acne and corrective lenses were absent now opening a strong friendly face to the world.

He sat behind a desk, which sat in a huge room that housed a bigger window and big screen television. There was a bookshelf holding books, a number of already-used diaries, and a couple of trophies. There were plaques all over the walls along with his educational diplomas. I followed the long trail of awards along the walls and came to a billiards table that sat to the right of a bright pinball machine. As I observed all of his wealth I had no realization of how to act so my knees and hands answered out in nervous shakes.

With a strange response he stood up to shake my hand, standing at an erect height, towering over me. I shot out my hand and shook his, with the simple expression of, hello Mr. Parker. After him, I took my seat, listening to the history of how his multi-million dollar corporation surfaced, and he owned every inch of it. He then began asking me questions to invade any bad work habits that may have been hidden, as if I weren't the biggest monster that haunted his nasty teenage years. The forgiven style he acted towards his largest fear adopted a chance of question that whispered out, maybe he had forgotten his torture during the wonder years, for I would have beaten me down if I were him.

He asked me if I were responsible as if he really had not known me and what I loved to fill my leisure time with. When I first entered the presence of Steve I thought for sure I would be declined of the employment with a revengeful escort that would heave me face first onto the front door pavement, but I somehow left his office untouched, and with a new job.

Though it was terribly dishonorable, I would be earning my desperately needed money as a filthy dark janitor. Working in the high school I once attended, next to people that typed on computers, which was all credited to a money-making program, invented by my new hated boss. I needed money and the huge disgusting sacrifice I ironically was thrust into was cleaning Steven's million-dollar fantasy of learning the technique of his past computer ways, and absorbing criticism from people like me, at my old high school.

I was now in demonstration of everything I labeled evilly and in a lame aspect, working my occupation with no consolations, but owning brown overalls that responded to my hands when they were covered with rancid human waste, smeared on the inside of clogged toilets.

I was trapped in the life of a loser but I was not fully there with my heart still growing towards the greater pleasures in life. I was intentionally avoided in the invitation from the productivity of parties, mostly because I worked such unwanted hours at a dignity-crushing job. While I work I observe some of the fine bodies of youth strut past me in newer fashions, as my looks tread in agony from the brown splashes of human defecation, forcing the opposite sex walk past me unnoticed and not admired. I sleep on the ground and can never afford the taste of my favorite drug because I continued to establish payment on a cheap apartment. I still haven't moved in because of the truthful dark knowledge that secretly flourishes inside of my thoughts, tell me that I live with my only friend. I live with the friend that I once rejected because of popularity that I once possessed, but currently do not. I can't even afford a couch or bed to put in my apartment. I can admit it now, as I push a smelly mop discovering what destiny has stored for its humble servant; I was living the life of a nerd, but I was not fully there yet. I still believed in a life of a greater style and I also still had the motivation of a winner.

I worked in my school for about a week when I finally heard from my sorry employer. He explained his mission in determining how his freshest employee was

127

valuing his job, as he again showed no revenge towards a piece of his painful past. Instead, Steven asked me what I planned to conduct myself in this coming weekend. Surprisingly, he insisted that I attend a church service then arrive to a party hosted by him. He gave me a card that had directions to his church and enscripted his address on the back.

I agreed on arriving because of one simple reason, I was forced to, my boss had all the disgusting blind power, which made me his slave and he knew it. I was also excited to enjoy the festivities in the forgotten episodes of partying. I disabled myself to be too overjoyed, remembering what type of person he was. It would be very pleasing to again witness my boss's reputation crush when he discovers that the public still despises his company. I would easily eradicate his reputation myself, if I weren't forced to clean after his teenage idolizing nerds.

That Sunday I put on my most decent clothes, and went to the prescribed church that my lame boss suggested. I can only say it was strange, as I entered a chapel flooded with people similar to my foolishly bizarre boss.

Strangers were introducing themselves to me in a very happy setting, and I saw hundreds of people hugging each other in joyous friendship as I tried to remember church when I was a carefree child, blocking out all of this absurd atmosphere. I hurried in, locating a chair sitting directly in front of two pretty faces that also counted for the only two civilized individuals in the strange worshipping coliseum. I watched all that appeared in this peculiar house of God, again trying to remember similar churches I once went to, establishing the difference and convincing myself to see how silly it was or how similar it was to my old church. I looked up to see the white hanging overhead background when Steven interrupted my sight, shaking my hand as if he was glad to see me here. He complimented me again and sat near the front, where the podium was.

After awhile a man walked up and began singing which triggered everyone else to sing in the praises of God. People then started to stand to their feet and clap then lift their hands up. It was a very silly place, in that memoirs of such an over jubilant atmosphere were never accounted for in past church experiences. After a long period of these happy gestures we all sat and rested, to listen for guidance that came from the preacher's lips. He announced Steven's name in demands of stepping up to the podium, which was not that puzzling, but it kept my concentration sprawled to his actions. Steven strutted up there with one hand holding a pretty young blonde that cradled an infant. I could not recognize Steven's elegant piece from where I sat, but once they plastered Steven's family through the overhead device, I was involuntarily sickened by the standing presence of the memorial figure that once destroyed a small part in me. It was the only girl that tamed my compassion. The only person I honestly proposed my love to. The last female I would have liked to lose to the dark lame freak that governed my place of employment.

There they were, standing beside each other loving their new created child, while passing proud expressions towards everyone watching. The inspiration of violence raged in my head to a dizzy disorientation. I dropped my head trying to conceal the unbelieving reality that unfolded before me. I could have passed out if I hadn't hid my eyesight away from the signature of hatred, back to the younger aged memories that anointed my brotherhood of everything suave.

The preacher blessed the child then blessed the child's mother, Jennifer, to a future of good health, love, and a better relationship to God. The crowd cheered for the miracle of birth, as the two sweet gossip speakers sitting behind me announced how fabulous they looked together as a family. The crowd carried on their applause, as Jennifer stepped out of the spotlight taking her seat, while her successful husband stood at the podium to give his testimony.

Currents of torture struck at my head as I sat and listened to a phenomenon speak to an audience that oddly accepted his mere presence.

The two ladies started again with their compliments, eavesdropping on what they wanted to do, I rejected any feelings to flirt with them after the service. Sweat rolled down my head, while they traded whispered phrases of sexual abuse that was directed not to me, but the childhood punching bag that once belonged to me. They detailed his great looks and his economic balance in every degree, as I attempted to impair myself of their sexual desires that pertained to the freak.

I could of stood up at that second causing a memorable scene, screaming at the two gossip speakers in a vulgar reminder that this gorgeous stud is truly the pathetic punch line of every high school joke.

Finally, I was given mercy as Parker stepped down then finishing everything said by the two followers sitting at my rear.

When the service ended I departed this spirit-crushing experience without talking to anyone else. I had to get out, I didn't wait for the bus, I walked home. I walked along the hot street when a nice looking BMW pulled directly in front of me, offering a ride. How great it felt to be given pity in such a troublesome time. I imposed on the nice stranger to open the black tinted door. I slowly slid open the side entrance to the disgusting smiling agitator of all my madness. Steven sat grinning demonstrating a high level of kindness, as he offered his biggest discomfort a free ride. Knowing Steven, he was probably trying to show off his wealth disguised as a good deed.

I did not want to, but I was forced to accept a ride, listening to every agonizing story my boss had about his kid, all the way home. I looked at him as he focused on the passing highway, so much wanting to rip out his throat, disabling him of speech. I watched him constantly yap as he began drawing near to the subject of his party and what high speculations it would bring.

Dropping me off, he explained the estimated head count and the only reason to attend alcohol. I was fixed on a line of desiring to go and refraining from the crowded celebration, but once again I was forced to.

Mr. Parker transported me back to Bradley's mobile settlement and immediately explained how he would be expecting my company delivered to the party. I let out a false thank you and entered my puppet's domain, about to ready myself for the socialized gathering that could only be achieved on time if I left in the next two hours. I would borrow transportation from the local bus system the majority of the distance, then painstakingly walk the rest, with the transit's awkward time schedules. The trip alone would at least take three hours without some type of car and also because of all the miles of walking.

As I started to prepare myself suitable I discovered a note attached to the counter in the kitchen. It brought me to my attention that I had the entire trailer to myself for the next three remaining days and that my favorite couple was out on vacation. Where, I hadn't known but I was extremely glad to finally be alone, without the moans and screams of naked satisfied soul mates.

After a moment of dressing myself and making a meal I motivated my actions to the long unwanted journey. My age was responding back with all of my stopping rests and aching bones, but it was made up with the consolation of arriving at the given address.

His house was gigantic, a true aspect of a mansion. He owned all the property that was lining the street. It was filled with a swimming pool, tennis courts, horse stables, and an area to ride them in, but it was the house that amazed me. It was dark out by now so I couldn't clearly make out the color. All I knew was that this towering mansion shouldn't have been wasted on such a man. There was a long black gate surrounding an infinite amount of grass and I had to use the intercom in allowing myself access to step into it. After I received my access authority, cars were pulling in, driving past me as I slowly walked. I was marveled when I passed a butler holding open the front door to an elegant familiar view. I could have easily told myself I saw this exact sight once before. I saw this uncanny familiar scene at my house when I once desired to create a painting. I had to make myself believe my eyes were not deceiving me for a sight that was so beautiful should not have spawned from the touches of a lesser being. It was, sad to say better than my old partying masterpiece.

I walked in and there were the same exact people that once engaged drinking festivities at my house dancing in the same rhythm only matured and dressed properly stunning. I recognized the veteran drinking brotherhood tossing up a quarter over by a huge old wooden dinner table that sat about ten laughing and giggling people. I focused my attention past them and into a room with the doors fixed open and observed old fellow party animals, playing a game of pool. To my right I witnessed the old traitorous drinkless designated drivers filling themselves at this party and not mine. Straight up, there was a huge sparkling chandelier, and also a staircase ahead of me that went up then split leading in both directions, spiraling around. Lovers were looking down on top of everyone from the safety rails, every once in awhile kissing each other in drunken turn-ons.

Steven was in no doubt trying to make me jealous but I declined in having my feelings manipulated in such a way, so I asked the nearest butler if he could make his pathetic existence useful and retrieve me a bottle of vodka. I realized that any servant of my hated boss could not do any task as easy as retrieving me an item so I followed him. As the legion of people I once knew very well failed to recognize me or just rejected the jubilant gestures of hellos, they probably grew out of.

I followed the butler into a large kitchen filled with cooks making small appetizers and exotic drinks. There were four chefs all working together as fast as they possibly could. The butler yelled to one of the cooks in handing him a bottle of my long waited drink.

One of the cooks opened a cover above him, then grabbing a bottle throwing it to the lazy butler that was supposed to retrieve it himself. The servant turned around to say something but I jerked the bottle out of his hand and immediately left his sight. I walked myself over to a crowd of familiar females to socialize in what has been accomplished since high school. I opened and drank straight from the bottle basking myself in the liquid heaven, finally enjoying the first taste of liquor that has not been absorbed in months, while listening to the tight pair of jeans announce she has fulfilled nothing, then quietly ending the conversation with evacuating my sight. It seems that the pretty face lost her inspiration to flirt and flatter myself naked, but it was no loss, with my attention now focused on another recognized walking pleasure. With my short mission set on conversing with this attractive piece, I again gulped down the burning feeling of my first love. As I started to talk to an old girl that wanted me, it was as if she did not recognize me and tried to give clues in talking to another. Her importance was completely exaggerated, as she thought of herself in a higher rank, interrupting my flattering words by responding to another male. Oh, it was a strange sight of conceit, watching this worthless piece turn away from me in an act of dominance. A new class of people had just fixed themselves on the long list of losers; they were the nobodies who believed themselves higher than me. They acted civilized and mature but concealed the monster within. They equaled nothing.

Trying to talk with the opposite sex started to become very annoying and frustrating, but she was a mere female with no special qualities. There were hundreds of premium girls here and instead of being the figure of introduction I thought I would live out my old days of effective female attraction and allow them to react to me. This would also distinguish a better period to access the forgotten leisure time activity of consuming alcohol peacefully. I sat down on the first step of his huge staircase and rested. As time progressed on I watched the world alone and drank. I knew Steven desired to arouse my jealousy inside with his expensive home and parties, but I could not have been more pleased with one of my favorite drugs, working in my body to the fullest. I was partly angry as I observed my once worshipping classmates walk by me with an absent hello, acting like I was unrecognizable, but with my growing maturity and aged face they probably didn't. I felt the anger rise up inside of me to the point of violence, so I left this pointless hangout area and decided to explore Steven's undeserved mansion.

I focused my destination upward, realizing how many have passed me in the last two hours. His staircase went up and then branched off in the opposite direction, spiraling all the way up. I went to the right until I came to an endless hall of doors. I checked the doors but most of them consisted of unused bedrooms, occasionally accidentally walking in on two drunken lovers in climax. There was a study in one door, with a large selection of reading material, but it failed to impress me. I opened the door to the next room and saw a glass display case that covered an entire wall. Inside was a stack of standing diaries and glistening gold trophies with inscriptions of Steven Parker. There were more then a dozen of trophies awarded to him, on the walls were plaques and framed newspaper articles also written about the freak. I was fixed on all his framed accomplishment thinking how could something so incredibly great happen to someone so pathetic. He did not deserve all this wealth and glamour. He was the lowest of the low and I was everything. It was a complete accident faulted by something supernatural and it was supposed to be given to me.

It was then I discovered one of Steven's personal diaries opened and unfinished. I began reading the first sentence only to find that my enemy had been creating passages about me I continued reading out loud, but to myself.

Dear Diary,

Today I invited my friend Mic to church. He didn't seem impressed, but I feel like I helped save another from the torments of hell. I hope he wasn't jealous when he saw Jennifer. I also gave him a ride home and invited him over tonight. I hope he comes, and if he doesn't may God help him.

The whole room was a horrible lure that failed to make me jealous. Only an obsessive loser would go out of his way to make others feel uncomfortable. What if Steven hated someone else with less confidence than I, the freak, would definitely destroy that person.

It was then and there when I realized just what I had to do. I took the empty bottle of Vodka and threw it against the glass, shattering it to my pleasing. I stumbled out the door and ran to find the twisted individual that caused me all this lost misery and anger. I came to the top of the stairs and watched the huge party from above, looking for the one person I wanted to confront, but couldn't. Not locating him I took the first step down and tripped, falling down each step in an embarrassing drunken tumble. I felt nothing, the alcohol in my system numbed my body enough, but not enough to block out the painful ridicules of the now watching and laughing crowd. After I got my head focused enough to regain my stance, I looked up to the friendly but hated face of Steven Parker. He was bending over extending out his hand in a peculiar unwanted help. I hated him for trying to help me but I was ecstatic to finally find my goal, it was time to set him straight, and I was more than happy to give it to him. I slapped his hand out of the way and stood to my feet, watching his smile turn to a questioning smirk. That's when his wife ran over, grasping his hand in a trusting acceptance, as she looked at me, asking how I have been. That's when I looked at Jennifer's greedy face and told her, I was doing much better than she will ever be. I then stared straight at the nerd's face and publicly explained how pathetic he was. I began pushing Mr. Parker and daring him to attack me, but as the freak stands he did not. He retaliated in the same fashion as he always did, by cowardly standing in observations of me punishing him. I spat in his face then began screaming my insults towards all of his belongings and accomplishments. I made him aware of how none liked his wealth and brought up how extremely hated he once was. He was trying to make me jealous and I established his knowledge of it by asking if he was. I remember this moment to the perfect detail as Steven's lips slowly opened to answer my question. He grinned at me and said, "I don't want you to be jealous, friend." I was glad because I was not jealous and made it known, then telling him how snobby he was, thinking his house and wife mattered.

I also remembered my next move as I grabbed his

wife's hand and announced her as the world's biggest slut, and that is when it happened. One second I was staring at the freak's ugly face and then I caught a flashing picture of his fist striking me between the eyes. I woke up in front of the black gate that outlined Steven's property and started to walk home in sorry defeat.

It was yesterday when that horrible wake up call occurred. I am presently still intoxicated, enjoying a few days alone in Bradley's trailer. I am lying face first on the kitchen's cool linoleum floor and I have just explained a long chapter in my incomplete life in a matter of seconds even though it probably seemed days or even months.

I can't move because of extreme exhaustion and my stomach has not tasted nutrients other than the three cases of beer I drank, after the party. I am lying in vomit and I can't establish my need of going to the restroom, but I know I have to go.

How pathetic I am. I could leave and no one would care for my disappearance. I am the full side of cruelty, facing punishment from all the slaves that overthrew my dictating power. I am nothing, and I wish I deserved the privilege of a quick bullet through my head, but I don't. I am serving a sentence from some supernatural force that has ironically given me every aspect that I had once also given out. I now realize where I am positioned in my sinful life. I am a geek, loser, nerd, moron, or reject. I have no desires and qualities to better this world. I am the exact opposite of popularity, but I wasn't always. I am pathetic and I would serve a greater purpose as fungus growing off the manure of some passing animal. I am now a loser and there is nothing that can prevent myself from being anything else. I am the face of everything different and weak, popularity led my life and now has crushed upon me so hard there is no need for hell because I am already there.

Dear Diary,

It is Thursday and I have finally found out what happened to my good friend Mic. The police officers told me that his death was unsure, but said a good estimation would be that he died of poison, exhaustion, hunger, thirst, and the lost will to live. I feel partly responsible with me knocking him out, but my wife says I shouldn't be. I love Jennifer so much and I am so proud of her. She said I'm a good human being in that I have never fought back at Mic until someone else was in harm. I wish I had prayed a little bit more for him and then everything would have turned out ok. I'm afraid to admit it, but I can almost see Mic spending his time in the worst place imaginable, but as he is receiving his punishment I will continue praying for his forgiveness. We all make mistakes and Mic was not a bad person at all, he just enjoyed life. I should have tried a little harder, but I know I will be forgiven. I am so glad I have such a great life and family to experience it with.

Yours Truly,
Steven Parker